FADE TO BLACK

P A WILSON

Ebook ISBN: 978-1-990509-07-0
Paperback ISBN: 978-1-990509-09-4
Audio book ISBN:978-1-990509-08-7

FREE EBOOK

Claim your copy of Running the Game when you use the QR code below to sign up for my newsletter and cheer on Pen as she vies for a commission in the military.

FREE EBOOK

Claim your copy of Running the Game when you use the QR code below to sign up for my newsletter and cheer on Pen as she vies for a commission in the military.

1

———

Sofie approached the doorway to the Open Pit pub. Like every commercial site on the Mallet, the doors stayed rolled up during business hours. And the Open Pit was always doing business.

She wouldn't come here if she had a choice. If she didn't need the black-market meds, there would be only two reasons for a detective to come through the noise and stink of the Maintenance section to the bar: to arrest someone or to investigate a crime. But she had the Fades, and if the boss found out, she'd be fired for putting her team in danger. So, illicit meds and unsavory locations were her fate.

Dr. Bindes was at his usual table. He was here most days for at least a couple of hours. There were official medical clinics in the Maintenance section, but they kept records. If you needed too much attention, you were too expensive and you would find yourself downgraded to a Manufacturing job — most people didn't last long in those roles. So, Bindes supplied off-the-books aid.

The Open Pit was about the size of ten residential quarters. Filled with long, black plastic tables and cheap, gray plastic chairs, there wasn't much privacy to be found in the pub. But Dr. Bindes sat at the far end of the left-hand table, no one around him within hearing. And by some kind of tradition, no one faced the table either. That agreement didn't extend to Sofie until she was within his private circle. Eyes watched as she passed, expecting a raid maybe. As a detective, she didn't wear a uniform, but a good cop was more about attitude than armor.

"You're out of your meds already, Detective Allen?" Bindes asked.

He was old even for someone in the Support caste. The higher you were on the ladder, the longer you might live. No guarantees, even for the Elites at the top. In space, shit happened, and it didn't care how powerful you were. Somehow, Bindes had lived to be old enough to look wise. Sofie wasn't convinced that working a medical black market to keep the lower castes healthy was real wisdom.

She didn't care. She needed the meds and the secrecy.

"Running low," she said, taking the chair to his right. From there she could see the whole room. "I don't want to run out on the job. Hard to keep an attack secret."

"I can get you the operation on the quiet. Then you won't have to visit our humble bar as often."

The operation would fix the condition, but it was risky, and she didn't trust that it would be completely private. "Just the meds."

He opened his hand and showed her the packet of caplets. "I only have a few days, but I can get more."

Sofie took the package and slipped it into her back pocket. "How much?"

Bindes looked around to see if anyone was paying attention. Sofie didn't need to check. She was always on alert.

"Nothing but a favor," he finally said.

"I'm not that kind of cop." There were plenty of cops he could buy to let him operate his side business — probably had already. "I'll pay cash and keep our agreement like always."

She reached for the credits tucked in her inside pocket. Bindes shook his head.

"The favor is nothing you will want to refuse," he said. "Things are odd these days. Don't you feel it?"

"Nothing unusual," Sofie answered. "The normal grumbling from the lower castes and complaining from the Elites and Executive." To be honest, she hadn't been paying a lot of attention to the mood of the station.

"Not unusual yet," Bindes said, "but something is bubbling. If there's a riot, I will need protection."

Unrest was the norm on the huge ore processing station known as the Mallet — officially designated Station 51. There were occasional large-scale fights down in Maintenance and Manufacturing — far from the Elites living on the top levels — but the punishment for interrupting commerce was severe. The docking bays on each end of the rectangular station were busy all day, taking in the ore and raw materials at the front and sending product out on transport ships at the back. The main purpose of the station was to collect, process, and ship the products of the mining operations in the system. Officially, at least. The unofficial purpose was to skim as much as possible without getting caught. Some of the incoming material was for the maintenance of the station, but a good ten percent of the rest went into the credit accounts of the people running the black market.

The last time a fight turned into a full-on revolution was over a hundred standard years ago. In her forty-three standard years, Sofie couldn't remember any large-scale violence erupting. She hoped to never experience it. But when your home got its name from the way it pounded every drop of hope and kindness out of its inhabitants, no one believed in peace lasting for long.

"Where's the trouble?" she asked. "I can go take a look."

"You'll need to take your partner," Bindes said. "Little thing like you needs a big backup."

"Fuck you," Sofie said, not taking offense at the poke about her lack of height. Tall or short, didn't matter in her job. Results were all anyone cared about. "I usually need to protect Rick, not the other way around."

Bindes laughed. "You are smarter than him, true."

"I'll tell him you said that." Sofie stood, preparing to head to the bullpen and start her day.

Bindes touched her arm. His humor gone, he said, "Don't go anywhere alone if you can avoid it. You might be able to take care of yourself, but everyone needs a partner these days. If only to pull you out of a fight."

Or prevent one? It was rare for a cop to get into trouble anywhere on the station, but it did happen. Two cops? She couldn't imagine a situation where it would be worth the risk. Attacking a cop was death. No trial, no appeal, no waiting. A partner would set his weapon to fatal and shoot before even thinking about calling for help.

"I'll be careful," she said. "But I have to do my job, just like everyone on the station. No passengers, right?"

Bindes nodded. "Not every cop has your condition. Don't let that slip your mind. You are vulnerable if you have an attack."

"I know. Thanks for the meds." She turned, glared at the other patrons like she was thinking of arresting everyone, and stalked out. After all, a cop had a reputation to maintain. And she wanted them all thinking her presence had been official so they wouldn't start wondering why she needed to see the doctor, and start planning how to use it to their advantage.

2

———

On her way to the office, Sofie tried to assess the mood of the crowds in Maintenance. It wasn't something she usually did because trouble just seemed to come toward her, so there was no point in going looking for it.

It did seem like she got more than the normal ration of shifty looks as she passed. But it could be that thing where you notice something because you're paying attention. Dangerous when a cop started focusing on normal activity like it was unusual; the wrong conclusions started to look completely right. Shifty looks from the lower castes were normal and the small groups bitching about life in the dark corners weren't out of the ordinary. She shoved the thought of riot and unrest into the back of her mind. If there was a problem, it would show up soon enough.

The office was close to the edge of Maintenance, the largest section of the Mallet. It covered sixty percent of the lower level and was broken into two parts; well, it more melted together about halfway through. The first section was dedicated to any work needed to keep the Mallet running, the second to maintain the processing equipment. The remaining space on the lower level was given over to the Support and Administration castes. The Manufacturing section was a darker, dirtier, more desperate version of the Maintenance one, and where ninety percent of the criminals on the station lived. Crimes committed by the higher castes were never put through official channels — unless some Elite wanted a more public punishment of an underling. Few people cared what happened in the Temporaries section at this end of the Mallet, since the residents were employed and policed by off-station corporations. The people living there did what they wanted as long as it fed money to the Elites, or at least didn't get in the way of the Elites making money. The dark streets also lurked in Maintenance, not far from the entrance to the Temporaries. A blot of streets and squares where no cop went without backup.

The bullpen was full of cops. Her partner, Rick Holdom, was talking to Amanda Mwendwa, an ambitious cop who saw Sofie as a rival. Sofie couldn't be bothered to tell her that she had no interest in promotion because the competition with Amanda kept her sharp. Her condition meant she was safer staying among the crowd of cops, rather than exposing herself to the scrutiny placed on the bosses. Amanda was everything Sofie wasn't: young, tall, skinny, extroverted.

"What's on the board for today?" Sofie asked. Rick looked away from Amanda and then down to Sofie. It did feel sometimes like the rest of the bullpen was populated with tall, rangy people who had been picked for their appearance. But it wasn't true. Every cop in there capable of catching even the most competent criminal. And handling the political crap as well.

"They tied up the sabotage case," Rick said. "Nothing but worker incompetence covered up by a supervisor."

"I don't know what would be worse," Amanda said, "the station blowing up from stupidity or on purpose."

"We'd all be dead either way," Sofie said. "It doesn't matter why to a corpse. Did they both get arrested?"

Amanda laughed at her and returned to her own workspace.

"So neither?" Sofie asked her partner.

"Turns out the supervisor had a bit of leverage. No charges on her, and the idiot got demoted to Maintenance. Let's hope it's not on something critical."

"No guarantee." Everyone from Elite to Manufacturing lived with the threat of the Mallet failing any time, any day, without warning. People who lived on planets endured similar threats of earthquakes, wildfires, flooding, or whatever else land-bounders faced. Everyone on the Mallet shoved the fear into some dark corner and ignored it.

"Paperwork," Rick said. "Maybe an early day? I have a new date for tonight. She's a singer."

"You're on a musician kick these days," Amanda said. "Your last partner was a drummer, wasn't he?"

Listening to gossip about Rick's love life wasn't going to keep Sofie awake. If she was filling out and submitting reports all day, Sofie was going to need a pot of stim-juice. "Boring might be nice for a day," she said. "You want coffee flavor?"

"Gives me heartburn. I'll take orange." He flicked on his monitor and pulled his pad off the charger.

Sofie poured two mugs of the clear stim-juice, then stirred in a caplet of the orange gel for Rick. Apparently it wasn't named for the color, but for some old Earth fruit. It was too sweet for Sofie. She opted for the tang of Rellian blufroot.

At her workspace, she turned on the computer and plugged in her pad. Rick liked to edit the contents of his notes on the pad and then upload. She preferred to get the data into the network right away and then clean it up. She'd seen Rick's idea of note-taking and wondered if the network would even recognize it as standard words.

"Allen, Holdom, get in here," the boss yelled over the speaker on Sofie's desk.

Sofie locked her screen but left her pad uploading information. "Why does he yell?"

Rick shoved his pad into a drawer and rose to join her. "Maybe he thinks we can't ignore the volume?"

The boss had an office with a door. It was glass and everyone could watch him work if he didn't turn on the privacy mode. The door had his name etched halfway up — *Captain Leif Llewelyn* — like people would forget it and need a reminder before they entered.

"Sit," he said when they stepped into the office.

He was old, or took pains to look that way. Despite his yelling and frequent blustering, Sofie knew his history. He'd taken down more than his share of criminals in his career.

"What's on your slate for today?" He didn't look at either of them, his attention on what must have been a report displayed on his desk pad.

Sofie told him and waited. Never offer any extra information, it just clouded the issue. And he didn't care anyway, or he'd have checked their schedules.

"An Elite got himself murdered. I'll have the files and details from the crime scene team in an hour." Llewelyn looked up and addressed Sofie. "Clear your desks and be ready. I want my best on this."

"Always up for a challenge," Rick said. "Is there anything we need to do specifically?"

Sofie let Rick do the talking while she thought through the implications. Wanting his best on this ass bullshit. Llewelyn said that kind of thing to everyone. He wanted them for a reason he couldn't say aloud. She hated reading between the lines.

"The crime scene team were sent first. Not by me, so don't start bitching. Someone is controlling the investigation. I'll find out who and get them off your back. I'll call you when I have something for you."

They'd been dismissed. Sofie followed Rick back to their desks. Her mind was spinning around the problems they already faced. The first on the scene was always a cop. They kept records of who entered the scene and gathered names and preliminary statements from any witnesses. Too much could have been lost already.

"You have anything on your desk to clear?" Rick asked.

"No. And Llewelyn is well aware of that. When did you get your weapon serviced last?"

"Yesterday, he knows that too. You?"

"This morning. Probably why he picked us?"

"I hope we don't regret being ready," Rick said. "My gut is telling me this is going to involve more than just a murder. And there's no way Llewelyn is going to protect us from interference."

3

Sofie sat back from the terminal and stretched. The new case was still a mystery — and that was a problem. Crimes were reported and investigated. There was no other process to go through. Unless the politics were complicated beyond the usual.

Her hand twitched as she released the stretch. Because she'd just spent an hour editing all of Rick's reports? Or was it the first twitch in an attack? One symptom didn't mean anything was wrong. She'd taken the meds on the way from the Open Pit. She formed a fist and the twitching eased.

"It's nice to see you so at ease." The voice was cultured and soft. Haadiya Rothwell, tall, handsome, young, and not to be trusted.

"Won't last long," Rick said. "Something is headed our way."

Haadiya nodded, his eyes flicking to take in the whole bullpen. Sofie kept her attention on him. His position as the Executive liaison to the Elite Sato family helped him gather useful tidbits of information. He was Rick's contact, but often gave Sofie the details if he wasn't around.

"Yes," Haadiya said. "I am aware of this incident."

"You have anything for us?" Rick asked. "We don't have it officially yet, but it's always good to have a head start."

"You must wait for the official word," Haadiya said. He flicked a gaze around the room again.

Nothing had changed. No one sat near enough to overhear their conversation. Amanda was the closest, and she was on the comm-link. Haadiya always made a big deal about security. Sofie's own contact, Nhu Eckerman, the liaison to the Ruiz family, was much more straightforward. Sofie couldn't help suspecting Haadiya put on an act for them. He behaved as if he was important enough to have enemies everywhere looking to attack him, but no one would cross an Executive for fear of retribution.

"I came to say this is complicated and you must strive to find the right solution. And find it fast."

Rick wasn't asking questions. *Leaving it to me?*

Haadiya wouldn't be here if he only wanted to issue a warning. The comm-link worked well enough for that and could be made secure.

"Is there a wrong solution?" she asked. "I mean, someone committed some crime. Our job is to find that person and turn them over to the judges. Seems pretty clear."

He gave her a smile that carried so much superiority she wanted to walk away. Only the chance he might have good information kept her from turning her back.

"There are crimes and perpetrators, and there are victims. In this case, your victim is the complication. It is vital that you start the investigation with the right goal in your minds."

Sofie looked away before she said anything that could

get her reprimanded. Insulting anyone of a higher rank was an infraction worthy of dismissal. It was possible that Haadiya wouldn't report her. He must like their interactions because he turned up on a regular basis, but she couldn't take that risk. She needed to keep this job. She wouldn't survive in Maintenance or Manufacturing with her condition.

"Thanks for the heads-up, Haadiya." Rick stood, his height making Haadiya look up. Not an insult unless the Executive decided it was. "We knew it was different. I'm sure everyone will be satisfied with our result."

Again, Haadiya scanned the room. "If you require any help, I have been assigned as your liaison to the Sato family in this matter. Please take advantage of the offer. I can clear the way for you."

He turned and strode out of the bullpen. A heavily built man in dark clothes stepped in beside him as he hit the walkway.

"Does he think we're incapable of reading the subtext?" Sofie stood and picked up her canteen. "I need a refill. You want anything?"

Rick was still staring out to the walkway. "No. I'm good."

"You think he meant something else?" Sofie asked. "I don't trust him, but..."

Rick shrugged and turned back to her. "He knows we aren't naive. I don't think he was talking about the case. Or not the crime we'll be assigned to. It was a warning to keep our findings to the reported crime."

"Something more than the usual skimming, graft, and corruption?" No crime on the Mallet stood alone. Everyone had their petty secrets, and as long as they didn't threaten the safety of the station, no one minded.

"We don't need this," Rick said. "We never do. One day we'll get a case that doesn't come covered in slime."

Sofie laughed at the idea that the Mallet would clean up its act enough to make Rick's prediction come true. Hell was hell, and it never got any better for the people doomed to live there.

4

————

Sofie made a new pot of stim-juice, added flavor to her cup, and returned to her workspace. This was the first time she'd been between cases, paperwork caught up, waiting for news.

"Allen, Holdom, Mwendwa, my office, now." The bellow came from Captain Llewelyn.

Why not just me and Rick?

Sofie let the others get ahead of her. That way she'd be the closest to the exit if the captain wanted to yell at someone. Not that she'd slip out, but it was nice to have the option.

"Shut the door," Captain Llewelyn said. "This is for you three only. Sofie, you're lead. Rick, do your usual thing as her partner, and Mwendwa, you're the backup."

"Why do we need a backup?" Sofie asked, the fear that he had somehow learned about her condition screeching in the back of her mind. He thought she'd have an attack in the middle of the case.

No. If the captain knew, she'd be off the force. Lying

about something like the Fades put everyone in danger. There was no predicting what she'd do during a blackout.

"This is high profile. You'll understand when I give you the details." The captain hit a button on his pad and the blinds sealed.

Sofie felt the pressure on her ears that signaled a sound-proof space. No one would be looking in, and no one would hear even if they lurked outside the door.

Rick took a chair and leaned back casually. "Okay, I guess it's going to come with all kinds of interference."

Amanda sat in the other chair, leaving Sofie to lean against the wall. *Fine with me.*

"Is this investigation supposed to be secret?" she asked. "It's hard enough to solve high-profile cases, but if we can't ask questions for fear of word getting out, then we have no chance."

The captain flicked an image onto the wall screen. A man, lying in a pool of his own blood — not a lot of it, but enough to confirm he was beyond saving. His black skin was already taking on the matte look of the dead. Sofie could see the door of a recycle chute. A service recess?

Sofie knew that face. "Oswald Sato? That's going to cause a shit storm until the new Sato Pratham is in place. Did the maintenance mech report it?"

"A tip, non-traceable. Now you understand," the captain said. "This level of privacy is for our protection. Just go ahead and investigate like normal. Well, maybe with a little more respect shown to the Elites."

"So, what happened?" Rick asked.

"Found early this morning shift. In the Maintenance section. Techs are done with the location. I ordered the body moved to the medical bay for autopsy right away."

"I like to see the scene first," Sofie said. "I guess leaving him there invites people to mess with the evidence while no one is looking." No one really liked any Elite, but Sato made a point of treating people like objects. The body would have been covered in excrement and urine within minutes of being found if it wasn't protected. "How bad was it?"

"We got the call fast enough," the captain said. "No one touched it, as far as the techs can see."

Seeing the body in place sometimes told a story. "Holos?"

"More than you need. They're all uploaded now. Some are still missing details, but I've been promised it's the top priority." The captain looked at her. "We've had this for three hours," he said. "I've been dealing with the Sato Second most of that time. The fight for Oswald's standing as Pratham is already getting vicious. You'd think the Elite families would figure out succession before it became a crisis."

The Elites like the bloodbath — literal and political. "Cause of death?"

"Not official, but the hole in his skull gives us a hint." He put another image on the screen. The body was turned on its side, the ragged hole in the back of the head already flaking with dried blood.

Amanda glanced at Sofie before saying, "He's big. It looks like someone took him by surprise. Or, maybe doped?"

The glance from Amanda before she spoke was a subtle dig at Sofie, hinting she wasn't asking the right questions. *She's a good detective. Maybe if she dropped all the infighting for promotion, she'd get somewhere.*

"Any chance it was from within the family?" Rick asked. "Wouldn't be the first time a Pratham was assassinated to create an opening."

Sofie wanted to get back to her desk and start assigning tasks. They weren't going to make any progress sitting here. "They would have hidden the body. Unless the killer wasn't a Sato. Maybe a Ruiz, or a Choi? Any of the nine families are capable. If an Elite is the killer, we'll be saddled with a scapegoat." Sofie pushed the idea to the back of her mind. It was far too early to start pointing fingers. "Is there anything else we need to know, sir?"

"I'm not going to tell you to be careful how you proceed. You already know this is going to be a fucking nightmare. I have two pieces of advice and one order. The order is to never leave me in the dark. I need to answer the questions I get from the other Prathams."

Sofie nodded. All the Elite families would be trying to take advantage of Oswald's death. The Sato businesses would be disrupted until the new Pratham was selected. Disruption meant opportunity.

"The advice?" she asked.

"Don't be afraid to ask the Sato Second for help. She'll want the crime solved quickly. Just remember she might not care if it's solved right. Keep Amanda apprised and use her."

The last bit surprised Sofie. It was no secret that Amanda didn't like her, but she thought she'd covered her own dislike well.

"Of course. I'm grateful to have the help." *And perhaps Rick can pair up with Amanda to keep her off my back.*

"Okay, dismissed." The captain released the privacy screening and turned back to his pad as though they'd already left the room.

Sofie reserved a case room as they walked back to their desks. "Meet me in room Alpha in five," she said.

By the time Rick and Amanda arrived, the crime scene images were displayed on the wall. The captain had been right about the number. Too many to make sense of in a short time.

"Amanda, you need to look through all the information uploaded from the techs. We can't deal with the onslaught."

"I can do the autopsy too," she said. "We need to be there when they cut him open, but I don't remember the last time it produced anything useful."

"Good. Rick and I need to talk to the Sato Second. I'll get that appointment. Then I think we need to go to the scene."

"I don't want to be stuck in here acting like an administrator," Amanda said. "I need to be out in the field."

That was why she never seemed to make progress in her race to a promotion. Sofie knew her own skills didn't lie in the political arena, but even she knew why Amanda was on the team.

"The captain thinks it's going to get violent," she said. "You're here to be ready to take over if one of us is injured. And someone needs to be the liaison between us and the Elites."

Amanda smiled at that. Making contacts at the top level would help her get somewhere. "Okay. Just keep me up to date, right?"

Rick stood facing the images flicking in and out on the wall. "I think you'll be keeping us up to date," he said. "You might find the answers in all this data."

5

The Sato Second answered Sofie's call herself. Not the normal wait of a few days to talk to a gatekeeper who would delay as long as possible before setting an appointment.

"I expected your call." June Sato smiled at Sofie from the monitor for a moment until she must have remembered the Pratham was dead, and she should only show contained sadness. At that point her expression went blank.

She was beautiful. Most of the Elite were, either from genetic manipulation or surgical intervention. Her dark skin was unwrinkled even though Sofie knew she must be middle-aged, somewhere around seventy years old. Running the administrative side of a powerful family put her in a position to alter the entire station's future. Probably why Seconds never ran for Pratham. The skills needed to grow the family businesses were very different from those to manage them.

"My partner and I need to meet with you," Sofie said. She was trying hard not to come across as someone frightened of power, but anyone who wasn't deserved to be shoved out an airlock. "We need some background. Nothing intrusive, I assure you."

"Perfectly understandable," June said. "I can be in the meeting space in fourteen hours."

That was three hours after their shift, but important cases didn't run on a regular schedule. She had plenty of meds, so no need to worry about having an attack.

"Thank you. Please send the link."

"Until tomorrow then," June said, already glancing away from the screen to something more urgent.

"That was fast," Amanda said without looking up from her pad. "Think it means she'll help?"

Sofie almost didn't bother to answer. Amanda wasn't naive, so she was probably testing Sofie. "I hope she doesn't get in our way," Sofie said. "That's helping, right?"

Amanda smirked and then lost interest in anything outside the contents of her screen.

"We should go look at the site," Sofie said to Rick. "Even with the body gone, we might see something helpful."

"The techs are still there," Rick said. "You know they won't let us near the scene."

Sofie couldn't sit still any longer. This was an important case and needed solving before the Satos started a war to find the killer.

"We'll see. But if we can't get close enough, we can try to find witnesses." Not that many people would be eager to point a finger at the killer — more likely they would be celebrating the death.

The comm-link flashed. Amanda reached for it, mumbled a greeting, and then snapped into perfectly straight posture. "Yes, she's here."

She handed the headset to Sofie. "Lilianna Ruiz."

The Ruiz Pratham. Shit. If every Pratham pokes their nose into the situation, the killer will never get caught.

"Ma'am." Sofie kept her words short and respectful. Not engaging with the woman was the safest way to get her off the call.

"Detective Allen." The voice was soft and gentle. A woman too refined to be affected by the evil in the world. Her image showed a delicate face, fair skin, fair hair, almost like some creature of the old myths of fairies and elves, but her green eyes were hard, ruining the effect. "I'm calling to offer my family's assistance, should you find it helpful."

Assistance? Yeah, more likely to be a spy or someone to shift suspicions onto a Ruiz rival. Otherwise, her Second would be calling.

"That is kind," Sofie said. "We currently have no questions or requests for assistance."

"Of course, you started the investigation only minutes ago."

The woman wasn't playing the same game as Sofie. Her next move was supposed to be a kind word and then the end of the call. She was fishing for something.

"There is one question," Sofie said. If she couldn't dodge the Pratham, maybe an attempt to get information would be fruitful — even if Ruiz just hung up.

"Anything," Ruiz said.

"Do you have any idea why someone would kill a Pratham? The Sato one in particular, or anyone in that position."

Hopefully something more than the fact that Oswald was rich, powerful, and nasty. Because that pretty much summed up every single Pratham, including the soft-spoken Lilianna Ruiz.

"I hope it is not political," Ruiz said. "The lower classes

are always dissatisfied. They are good people, I'm sure, but also envious of our position, and I hear rumors of a growing level of... discontent. The Sato family has fingers in all kinds of enterprises. They are... not selective in their business. Perhaps a partner?"

"Another Pratham?" Sofie let the question slip out without thinking. Was Ruiz trying to shut down another family by threatening their Pratham? Ruiz could be trying to prepare Sofie for some very high-level interference — the case already carried political weight. And did she really believe anyone living on the Mallet was ever content?

The laugh that came through the comm-link was a tinkle of delicate sounds. "Oh, I doubt anyone in my position would stoop to murder. Or, at least not such gross violence when a simple poison would do the job without raising suspicion."

Only someone so powerful as to be untouchable would make that joke during a murder investigation. The death of one Pratham might not be isolated. This unrest that Ruiz worried about, could it be a cover for something more serious?

"If you think it's a partner, do you know what business Pratham Sato was engaged in? Who the partner was?"

There was a long pause and Sofie wondered why Ruiz mentioned a partner when she wasn't ready to hand over names.

"I don't know," Ruiz finally said. "It shames me to say there is something important that I am ignorant of, but there it is."

"Then I thank you for your offer of help. We will keep it in mind as we follow the clues we find."

"I understand you are busy," Ruiz said. "Please contact our Executive representative, Nhu Eckerman, if you need anything. If your request is of a... delicate nature, you can use this comm code to reach me directly."

Why is she pretending I don't know who Nhu is? Now I can't trust my usual source of information because she's being manipulated. "We will. Thank you, Pratham."

Lilianna Ruiz ended the call with all the expected niceties.

"You ready?" Rick asked. "Or has the Pratham ordered you to do something?"

"Let's go. Maybe we'll get lucky and find this evil partner lurking in Maintenance, drooling over the evidence of his crime."

She gave Amanda and Rick a summary of the call and led Rick out of the bullpen.

"You think Nhu is going to screw us?" Rick asked. "You want to ignore them when they make contact?"

Sofie turned right into the passageway leading to the Maintenance area. "You trust Haadiya?"

"Never," Rick said with a grunt. "But he gives me some good leads. I just have to peel back a few layers of self-interest and deniability to get there."

"Same with Nhu," Sofie said. "They're just better at seeming trustworthy than Haadiya."

"Never had a Pratham involved in an investigation before," Rick said.

"Has anyone? I think she wants to throw a little shit on the Satos while they're vulnerable. If an Elite family is ever vulnerable." It was going to be hard to keep her mind on the crime with all the interference.

6

———

The Maintenance section was crowded. Sofie's shoulders itched with some undercurrent of emotion she couldn't identify. Not the fact that people kept brushing by her as they passed. No one added any force to the contact, it happened because of the number of people in the narrow walkways. Shift change was almost complete. Soon half of the bodies would be at work, and the other half home, or in a bar.

Nothing out of the ordinary here. Probably just the Ruiz Pratham's comments poking at her mind. "You feel anything weird?" she asked Rick, just to be sure she wasn't rationalizing away her fear.

He looked around and shrugged. "Busy but quiet. No one is yelling or preaching."

Maybe that was it. The quiet.

"Let's get to the scene. Did you contact the supervisor?" She shouldered through a knot of bodies into a less crowded space. Without the human scents, the stench of Maintenance hit her. Burned grease, solvent, and sweat. It hung in the air as if trapped by the humidity and heat. Sofie breathed through her mouth to minimize the impact until her nose could ignore the reek.

"Yeah, name of Mitch. He'll be there in thirty." Rick nodded toward a side corridor. "We turn here. The crime scene's pretty deep in the residential section."

In a service recess. The pictures mostly showed the aftermath of the crime. "What the fuck was he doing down here?" she asked.

She followed Rick closely, her hand on her weapon. The people loitering in this part of the ship were desperate. Vagrants fired for making mistakes, or just pissing off the wrong person, or because they were old or sick. They depended on the scant charity their neighbors could afford if they were lucky. If luck wasn't with them, most headed for the dark streets, where the desperate sold their bodies or facilitated depraved services. A few chose the recyclers as a way to end their misery.

A couple of men lounged in the shadows. They broke eye contact fast and slipped down another passage. She watched until she lost them in the gloom. There was plenty of power to keep the section well-lit, but residents broke the globes, and the Elite didn't care about the danger darkness represented.

"A coin?" The voice was shaky.

Sofie glanced at Rick's back. "Hold up."

She bent to look at the man slumped in the doorway of a store. Nothing about him was remarkable: dirty-blond hair, brown eyes, skinny in a way that hinted he'd never been heavy. Trembling hands, sheen of sweat, voice cracking. No reek of alcohol to explain his state. He was recovering from an attack of the Fades. "Why aren't you being treated?" she asked.

He reached for her hand, but Sofie shuffled back. He

probably carried some other disease or parasite along with the Fades that she didn't want to pick up.

"Why are you so sick?" she asked. Maybe dropping a few of her meds in his palm would help.

"The bosses got no use for me like this," he said. "No meds for them who can't work."

Fucking assholes. A cheap treatment, or a course of the meds and he'd be back to the job in a couple of days. "What's your name?" She slid her hand into her pocket and worked a few meds free from the bag. She'd just have to go see Bindes sooner than planned. Maybe tell him about this guy.

"Deacon." His eyes were on her movements.

Sofie checked Rick's position. He stood guard, casual but alert. His attention was on their surroundings, not her. "You see anything to do with the murder?"

Deacon stared at her pocket. "Don't see much of anything these days."

She removed the meds and showed them to him. "This should help you for a few days, maybe enough to get you back to work," she said. "You sure you didn't see anything?"

"Elite, right?"

Sofie nodded.

"Probably deserved it," Deacon said. "Saw the techs."

Sofie closed her hand on the meds.

He reached out again, his eyes moving from her hand to her face.

"You gonna leave me to die?"

By the look of him, it wouldn't be long before starvation took him.

"If I give you these, will you go to a shelter?" No one wanted to live in the shelters run by the Accept priests. You received the bare minimum to survive in exchange for constant preaching about accepting what their god placed on you as a burden.

"Rather die here," Deacon said.

"So what will you do?" Sofie opened her hand again. "You get a couple of days of functioning. Then this starts again."

"Who knows what will happen in those couple of days," he said. The smile he tried to force through the trembles was painful to watch.

"If you remember anything, you call me, right?" She dug out a contact card. "This only calls me, don't lose it."

She put the card in his outstretched hand. All he needed to do was press the image in the corner and her pad would signal the contact.

He nodded — or it might have been another bout of tremors.

"Put it away," she said. When he managed to slip it into a pocket, she dropped the meds in his palm.

She rose from the crouch and started to move toward Rick. Time to see what the techs left at the scene.

"Hey," Deacon called weakly.

Sofie turned. He beckoned her back. She stood out of reach and waited for him to continue.

"Didn't see the murder, but you be careful who you trust. Not just that dead Elite involved."

She looked at him. Was there a message she wasn't hearing? The words were useless to her. Of course there were more people involved.

"You take care of yourself," she said.

Rick straightened up when she reached him. "Anything?"

She stepped ahead of him to take the lead. Following

Rick meant he blocked her view of what was ahead of them. "Nothing."

"Too far gone?"

"Probably," she said. The image of her own body in the same state as Deacon's chilled her. One day she would have an attack she couldn't stop. One day her body would keep trembling and that would be the end. She might get the treatment, but even cured, the job would be gone, and she had no other skills.

"What did you give him?" Rick asked.

He didn't look at her, but the question slid an icy blade in her gut. No way Rick knew. If he suspected she was up to something, he wouldn't let it go. She couldn't let him find the truth. She couldn't be beholden to him to keep her secret.

"Some vitamins. Nothing to make him talk, if that's what you're asking."

He glanced down at her. "No. You wouldn't do that. You think vitamins will help him?"

"Probably not, but a kind gesture can make him more likely to trust us." She looked at her pad. "We turn right at the next junction. The scene is the second right after that."

Her original question came back. What was Oswald Sato doing this far from his pristine and elegant home? What would draw him down to his death in this section of the Mallet?

The answer might explain why he died, and who did it.

7

The recess where the body was found was poorly lit even for the neighborhood. Sofie plugged her pad into a port and turned on the light. Harsh, but maybe it would help.

"Not enough blood," Rick said. "He was dumped here."

Sofie looked around. Some blood, but yeah, not enough for the injuries they'd seen on the image in the captain's office.

"Let's look around first," Rick said. "I'll pop the holo down after."

The techs would be working on the evidence they'd pulled. A murdered Elite meant their case would be the top priority for the techs. The holo, evidence list, and preliminary conclusions would be updated in the system by the time she and Rick completed their own examination.

"It's been a long time since a mech came in and used this space. Someone must have altered the programing. Amanda can research it," she said.

A few spots showed tracks in the mud of blood, dust, and detritus. It had been so long that the mech tracks were covered with a layer of gunk and were only visible where the scene team had removed the top layer. The designers of the station had formed the metal floors to look like cobbled streets. Apparently, they thought the appearance of being on a planet might be good for the mental well-being of the inhabitants. Here, the cobbles were scraped down in places and some flat plates were bolted on. Perhaps that was why the recess was abandoned. Mechs would have difficulty traveling along such an irregular surface. If this represented the kind of service the Maintenance section received, no wonder people were restless.

"We can get the logs, maybe find out why it's disused. I think we're dealing with a local," Rick said.

Nothing special in that observation. Sofie kept scanning the floor and walls, hoping for anything the team might have marked. Not anything they'd missed; the team didn't miss anything. They didn't make guesses either.

"What did they find on him?" she asked. "I'm pretty sure this didn't happen because someone wanted to kill an Elite for a thrill."

Rick tapped his pad to check the draft report. "Nothing. No ID, no credits, no jewelry. Yeah, robbery might be a motive. Hard to fence that kind of stuff. Everyone would know who it came from."

"The Temporaries," Sofie said. "It's probably off-station by now."

Rick grunted like he agreed with her.

A green tag caught her eye up on the back wall. "The crime scene team are still recording." Maybe the killer came back or would come back. A faint hope, but if it happened they needed to capture it.

"Ten minutes for the holo update," Rick said after

checking his pad. "Report agrees this isn't our primary scene."

"Could mean we have more than one crime." Sofie stepped out of the recess and checked the passageway. Still quiet. How much activity could go on before someone got curious? It would take strength to carry Sato to the recess, or some kind of help. "Or two killers."

Rick was still scanning the reports, giving Sofie time to follow her own instincts. This neighborhood was empty after the shift change. Either everyone healthy enough to work was at work, or they were inside recovering for their next stint. No kids playing in the halls. No adults chatting or taking a walk. All the killer had to do was wait for the right time and no one would see them move the body. The kill scene couldn't be far though. The residential street might be easy to slip into without notice, but carrying a body any distance meant going through busier areas with witnesses.

"The holo is ready."

She turned away from scanning the area outside for clues to see a body sprawled on the floor of the recess. The Sato Pratham looked like any other murder victim, all power vanished with his life. That similarity ended with the body; the aftermath of a Pratham's murder could affect the entire station.

"He wasn't just tossed in," she said. "Someone placed his body. That took more time."

"Did you see anything outside?" Rick asked. He placed his pad on a ledge beside Sofie's and sprayed his shoes to protect any evidence still remaining. "Should I tell the techs to come back?"

Sofie treated her shoes and handed the dispenser back to Rick. "Ask if they've already done the passage. If not, it might be too late. There's been a shift change."

Rick sent the message and returned his pad to the shelf.

It was the same positioning of the body they saw in Llewelyn's office: Sato on his stomach, head turned to the side.

The holo showed Sato's head turned to the right, his arms placed like he was trying to crawl away, but he was facing the back of the recess. His legs were broken and turned at unnatural angles.

"Turn off the holo for a minute," Sofie said. "Let's see what was under him."

The body flicked out and Sofie moved to stand over the spot where Sato's head had rested.

Rick stepped across to the other side, as though the body was still lying there. "No scratches on the exposed skin visible in the holo, so he wasn't just dragged and dumped. The body might have been posed."

"We might get a hint about the actual murder site from the autopsy." She bent low to see the indents left by Sato's belt and buttons in the dirt coating the floor. "He was here long enough to make a mark."

"The report estimates a day." Rick moved to where Sato's feet had rested. "No drag marks. So he was carried."

"Either by more than one person, or a piece of equipment," Sofie said. "No, more than one person moved him for sure."

"Because of the posing?" Rick moved back to turn the holo on again.

"There's a dent in the muck here." Sofie pointed. "Like the toe of his boot hit here before they arranged it."

"Another mark here," Rick said, pointing to what looked like a slice in the coating. "He went in facedown. They turned his head."

None of what they'd found would help find the killer or

the original crime scene. Maybe there was trace on the body or the clothes to help, but it would be hours before the techs were done with their work.

"Is the holo complete?" Sofie asked.

"Not quite. You want me to turn it on?"

"Might as well. If there's nothing, we can talk to the residents."

"And the supervisor should be here any minute."

Rick touched his pad again. The body flickered and then settled with the underside showing. There were gaps in this view. The techs must still be putting data points in, to finalize their findings.

Sofie stared at the image. Very different from the first view. Now they could see his face was torn, like someone had raked a sharp fork across it. Not fingernails, too deep and regular. His hands had been sliced across the palms. His jacket and shirt were open. The same instrument had been used to lacerate his chest.

"Personal," Sofie said. "Someone hates him for who he is, not for his status."

"Fuck the stars." The voice came from the walkway behind them.

Sofie stepped out to the walkway, hands on her weapon. A man. In the dark-gray overalls of a supervisor.

"Mitch?" Rick asked.

"Yeah, do I need to see that?" Mitch pointed to the holo.

Rick turned it off and joined them in the walkway, the crime scene barrier snapping into place as soon as he stepped from the recess.

8

"We'll be talking to everyone who lives around here," Sofie said. "Where were you over the last day?" It was a pretty broad time span, but if they needed this Mitch to give a full statement, it wouldn't be in the back alley of his neighborhood.

"My job." He puffed up a little as he spoke. It didn't do much to enhance his appearance. The man was chubby, something few residents of Maintenance could hope to achieve. His weight might be from flabby muscles rather than fat; he looked like a young, retired ring fighter. Maybe he'd been injured badly enough to end that career. His hair was thin and stringy where it wasn't completely gone, his eyes a blue so pale it almost didn't register as a color. "Checking on people who claim to be ill. Making sure no one is loitering. Keeping the peace."

"You work twenty-four-hour shifts?" Rick asked.

It wasn't unknown for some jobs to run long shifts. The people worked on stims for up to two days without more than a half-hour break. Then they took downers to sleep. Those jobs burned people out, but they were all critical tasks. No one expected a supervisor to work more than a few hours in a row.

"No. But I'm either sleeping or out of my section if I'm not on the job. Don't like to drink with the residents."

More likely the residents didn't want to drink with him. He wasn't doing a great job of maintaining his part of the neighborhood. If he was, Deacon would have been in a medical clinic, not the doorway of a store. And there was no way the body would have been in the recess so long if he made his rounds. It was possible that Mitch took money to look away from certain activities. Since Deacon couldn't pay a bribe, he got ignored. It was also possible the man was just lazy.

"Did you call in the body?" Rick asked.

Mitch shook his head.

"So, an important man gets killed in your section, and you don't know anything about it?" Sofie asked. Rick could play it neutral, but she figured Mitch would react to her aggressive questions, and that would make him slip on something they could use.

The lie flicked across Mitch's face before he reconsidered. Even he had to know lying to the police would bring trouble, no matter if he was innocent of the crime in front of them. "Yeah. That's exactly what happened. You think I can be everywhere? Most of the time this section is empty. People work, eat, sleep. All kinds of shit could be going on outside their homes. No one snitches."

Rick took over. "Other supervisors have people helping to keep their homes safe."

"Yeah, and other supervisors don't have to deal with the same people I do. No one talks and everyone turns a blind eye."

"Anyone claim to be ill yesterday?" Sofie was tired of his whining. "Someone you didn't check on?"

"A few are sick. No one malingering," Mitch said. "No one can afford to lose a shift's pay down here, so they work unless they can't stand up at a machine."

"We need their names and unit numbers," Rick said. "We need the same for anyone sick on the previous shift too. We can get the rest of the names from the system."

Mitch pulled his pad out and sent the names to Rick. "Here's who's supposed to be living in each unit too."

"What do you mean, *supposed* to be living?" Sofie asked. "Residents don't move around without notice. There's nowhere to go."

People were assigned living units by their work shift. No one decided to move along —there were no unregistered units.

"I might be behind in updating the system. Had a few deaths last couple of weeks."

Possible, but Sofie figured there was some scam going on that gave Mitch a little spending money. Everyone on the Mallet had secrets and some people would pay to keep theirs.

"We'll check the official list when we get back to the office," Rick said. "Who's around now for us to question?"

"Shift just changed. I don't know who's out getting supplies or who came home. You might want to go back and check the list now."

So he would have time to clear out anyone who shouldn't be inside a unit? "We'll decide how to proceed," Sofie said. "When do you suggest we come back?"

"Give it an hour," Mitch said. He sounded relieved.

"Okay," Rick said. "This is just the preliminary state-ment. We'll need to talk to you again later in the investigation. Read this and sign at the bottom." Rick held his pad out.

"I didn't realize it was a statement," Mitch said. "I might need to add some stuff. Just to be sure."

Sofie loved this moment, when a person realized they were on the record. It made them more careful, and sometimes drew out information that helped the case. Even innocent people got nervous. She'd learned over her career that nerves didn't always mean guilt — just most of the time.

"Okay, it's good," Mitch said, and signed. "Do you want me to come back and help you interview residents?"

"No," Rick said. "Thanks for the offer, but we'll get started now, and I'm sure you have work to do." Rick checked the signature then turned the pad off.

"Okay. Like she said, you know what you're doing. Can you tell me anything about that?" He nodded his head toward the recess. "My residents will want to know if they're safe."

"We don't give out details on our open investigations," Rick said. "We'll contact you if we need to ask more questions."

Mitch still looked at the police barrier. It was opaque, and no one would be able to look at the scene or penetrate it.

"Your residents are probably a bit safer than before," Sofie said. "We'll be around for a while. Maybe the crime scene team too."

"Okay then." Mitch gave her one last look and then strolled away as though nothing was out of the ordinary.

"His list matches the official one," Rick said. "So, I guess he was trying to cover for a few people who might not have permission to be here? Weird that he believed we'd have to go back to base to check."

"Definitely something shady going on," Sofie said, watching Mitch turn the corner. "Not sure it's anything more than the usual petty shit."

"Let's try a few doors before we head out."

No answer at the first unit, or at any of the units in the small passage.

9

In the case room, Sofie felt her fingers tingle. The first warning of an attack of the Fades. The meds were wearing off hours too early.

Rick and Amanda were looking over the latest reports while she plugged through the list of residents, looking for any hint of motive. Or any hint of a different motive than the obvious: an Elite was where he shouldn't have been with no protection. Their attention might be captured enough for Sofie to slip a couple of meds in with a sip of stim-juice, but no guarantee.

She couldn't let the symptoms get worse. She couldn't take her meds here without Rick or Amanda asking questions. Rick was already suspicious about her story when she gave Deacon those pills.

"Back in a few," she said. The trip to the washroom would be fast, but she'd need a few minutes for the symptoms to disappear.

The captain's voice came over the intercom. "Allen, Holdom, my office."

Rick looked up. "Great. He's expecting a solution right now."

Fuck. Now she might not get to the meds early enough to prevent an attack. When the symptoms got past tremors in her fingers, the meds could only minimize the impact of the attack. If Llewelyn dragged out a meeting, she was done for.

Why were the meds failing?

"We have some bits," she said.

"You're in for a lecture or an ass-kicking," Amanda said. "I'll do a bit of snooping into the political mess while you face the consequences of ignoring it."

Just like you.

"Thanks," she said. "It's hard enough to get people to talk about the incident without having to worry who we're offending. Because someone is always disgruntled, right?"

Amanda grunted a laugh and picked up the comm unit.

"You need a minute?" Rick asked.

Sofie considered the risk of waiting to top up her meds. If she delayed with the captain, it would be bad. Her symptoms were still just the tingling. "No. He won't take long and then we can get back to the lack of progress we've made."

He gestured for her to lead the way.

The captain didn't wait for the door to close before he started talking. Not yelling, but not far off.

"What were you doing for so long at the site?"

"Talking to the supervisor, checking out some clues, knocking on doors." Sofie sat without waiting to be offered a chair by the captain. Rick slipped into the chair beside her. "The tech report is still in process, so we thought checking out the scene might reveal a clue."

Llewelyn glanced at his comm unit. The light flashed to notify him of an incoming call. He muttered something

Sofie couldn't make out, then turned his attention back to her.

"You talked to June Sato?"

"I have an appointment," Sofie confirmed. "I'm not briefing her on our progress. The investigation is not public."

"Unless you want us to," Rick said. "I'm not volunteering, but Mwendwa would love that kind of thing."

"Keep me updated and I'll take care of the Elite interference."

"How much detail?" Sofie asked. Her heart was slowing. She needed her meds within the next five minutes, or she would collapse, and her secret would be out for everyone to witness.

"Overview only," he said. "What did you find today?"

Sofie rubbed her fingers together behind her back. Maybe improving the circulation would buy her time.

Rick pulled out his pad like he needed to check the details. "We figure the killing took place elsewhere, but not too far from the recess. Can't carry a body around without someone seeing. We need to go back when the residents aren't working. We think his possessions might have been taken by someone after the body was moved."

"Good work. Any initial suspects?"

"There's something brewing in Maintenance," Sofie said. "It might just have been a crime of opportunity. Someone angry and drunk enough to think an Elite is asking for trouble if he's outside his section and alone." The tingling ebbed as her fingertips warmed.

"Not going to be enough to satisfy the Satos," the captain said. "Any chance this might be internal fighting among the Sato family or another Elite clan?"

Like the Ruiz Pratham? There wasn't enough in their

conversation to elevate Lilianna Ruiz to suspect. The tingling returned in a rush.

"Is there a preferred candidate for the Pratham?" Sofie asked. She hadn't seriously considered a Pratham hopeful would kill Oswald to create an opening for the position. It was a stretch. Elites didn't usually resort to physical violence, and if they wanted Oswald gone, no one would have found the body. "Or some rumor of business rivalries gone too far?"

The tingles weren't receding. Sofie slowed her breathing. Panicking would only bring on the attack faster. No trembles yet. She still had time. But the meeting needed to end.

"No and no." The captain sat back in his chair and glanced over Sofie's shoulder. "You talked to the Ruiz Pratham, right?"

"She called to offer her assistance. We know that means to interfere. Even if I believed her offer, I don't need that kind of help."

"Good. I need to hear as soon as any Elite gets in touch. I need twice-daily updates even if you haven't found anything new. I'll keep the politics away as much as I can, but this is going to attract the higher levels for all kinds of reasons. Not many of those reasons will be *about* the murder, but most will be *because of* the murder. Elites don't like it when someone else stirs their pot."

"Okay," Sofie said. "I appreciate the help."

"You sure you don't have any names yet?"

So someone can put them on a hit list? "Not yet. Maybe the tech report will point out something, or one of the residents will open up." She felt the first twitch of a tremor in her baby finger.

"We need to talk to the supervisor again," Rick said. "I don't suspect him, but I think he was hiding something. May be unconnected — there's enough shifty stuff going on in the lower levels to make him lie to us — but it's worth another go at him."

Sofie put her hands on the arms of the chair to push herself up. Her heart was so slow that she didn't think she'd be able to stand without the help. It also hid the tremors that would be visible if her hands were free.

"I have faith you'll find the truth," the captain said. "Between us, that's all we can hope for. Justice is going to be tricky to define here. Oswald Sato wasn't a good man — even for an Elite." He waved them out of his office.

Sofie hurried for the washroom instead of going back with Rick. Inside, she locked the stall and dry swallowed a med capsule. It took ten minutes for the symptoms to disappear. It was going to take hours for her body to recover from the strain and fear of the episode. And all that time she had to appear normal and healthy.

She walked into the case room to find Rick and Amanda spreading printouts along the table.

Rick looked up. "We've got the final images from the crime scene. It might help to look at them from above. Different kind of view than a holo."

"Good idea. Nothing much more to follow up on today. Let's get a look and then head out. We need to start early tomorrow to get to the residents before they head in for their shifts." *And I can sleep off the aftereffects.*

The papers only confirmed what Sofie thought at the scene. There was definitely not enough blood for that recess to be the murder site.

10

———

The drain on her energy from narrowly missing an attack sent Sofie into a deep sleep that night. Her comm woke her an hour before her alarm but she was fully conscious at the first sound. Grateful sleep could still restore her — because it wouldn't if the attacks kept coming — she checked the name of the caller. Nhu Eckerman, the Ruiz family liaison and her contact at the Executive level — and now another political angle to work around.

"Morning," Sofie said.

"I like that," Nhu said. "Not committing to good or bad."

"What can I do for you?" Sofie wanted to clean her teeth and do the rest of her morning routine. If she was up this early, she could get out and track the area residents to move ahead on the investigation. But Nhu was normally useful, their tips coming without the probability of betrayal or personal agenda. But Nhu was an Executive and that meant they couldn't be fully trusted.

"Yesterday Nhu left me a message for you."

Nhu was divided gender and lived the male and female

identities as different people. Sofie only saw Nhu's head and shoulders, so it was difficult to guess which gender was present today.

"And?"

"She noted that children are missing in the Maintenance section."

It wasn't unusual for kids to slip away. The older they got, the more they could get up to, so it could be days before anyone went looking.

"What do you know about it?" Sofie asked. "Is this shared information between you and Yesterday Nhu?"

"I am aware. She realized it was important. Women are much better at worrying about children."

"Are you going to share what you know? Sir." She added the last quickly. Nhu was Executive and expected respect, no matter how friendly they seemed, and if yesterday's Nhu was female, today's Nhu must be male. "Is it possibly related to the murder?"

"That is for you to determine."

She was too busy for this bullshit, but Sofie couldn't hang up. It was important enough that Nhu had passed it between genders. "What is the information?"

"This is not simply a few exploring and rebelling teenagers. The missing are small children. Ones unprepared to... protect themselves. And not for a few days, either. Permanently."

It was something. Maybe not related to Oswald's murder, but something that should have been reported much sooner than this. As far as the controlling Elites were concerned, children were the next generation of workers. If they were disappearing, then production would suffer in a few years. Nhu was right. Teenagers could protect themselves and often ran in packs. But children?

"How young?"

"Between three and five years old. All Maintenance brats. No other class is affected."

"Thank you, Nhu. We'll investigate. Do you have names?" It couldn't hurt to ask.

"She did not leave identities in the note, and I am not aware of the intimate details, simply the fact of the absences."

"We'll find out." Sofie reached for her clothes. It was more important now that she get into work and find out the truth.

"I'm sure you will," Nhu said. "There was one more thing. The she Nhu said your department already knows."

Fuck. "It will make it easier to start looking if we have records," Sofie said, keeping her reaction confined to her own head.

"I am asking you to remind your captain that he may not think the children of the Maintenance section are important, but they are. The Elites do not like to have their assets wasted."

Nhu ended the call.

It still disgusted Sofie to hear someone refer to people as assets.

Two minutes later she was clean and dressed. She took a med, reminded herself to track down Bindes to find out what the hell was wrong with them, and locked her unit door behind her. The case room was the best place to figure out the connections between the dead Elite and missing children.

WHEN SHE ARRIVED in the case room, Sofie was alone. Even with their lack of progress, the walls were cluttered with notes, ideas, holo-flats, and report printouts. It looked like chaos, but soon enough a little clue would help them see a pattern, and that would lead to their killer.

She found a blank space on the wall and projected her notes from the pad. It helped her think to have the data points displayed with the other information. If it came to anything, she could produce hard copies to be placed with the rest. For now, she kept her thoughts on her pad. Putting up a theory so early on was dangerous because it was too easy to ignore any clues that didn't match the theory.

She listed the items she knew.

Motive: greed, vengeance, petty rivalries gone out of control.

Suspects: Mitch the supervisor? A resident? Another Elite? Or someone hired by an Elite? This was the biggest reason for not posting the notes. If an Elite was a suspect, the case could be shut down to avoid embarrassment.

The missing children: Related? Motive? Where are they? Who are they?

Not helping.

She snapped the app closed and signed into the reports database. If the missing children were on file, she could find out what happened. She had a crawling suspicion that Nhu's implication that the reports of missing kids were being ignored was correct. The kids weren't important enough to merit the time of an investigator. Whether that was because the police didn't have enough resources, or they simply didn't want to bother looking for Maintenance kids, it didn't really matter. All that counted was whether the kids were found — or their bodies, at least.

The results of her search rolled across the screen. Forty kids between three and five years old reported missing from Maintenance families in the last six months. Forty was too many to be a coincidence. Sofie didn't know how many would be normal, but it had to be less than one or two in a month. And her gut said forty was too many for one crime. Her job was to find the link between the kids and the murder if there was one, not to find all the reasons children would go missing.

She transferred the list of parents' names to her pad. Time to go back to Maintenance and find out what exactly was going on before the whole thing blew up and more people were murdered.

11

This early in the day, before shift change, Maintenance was quiet enough to feel eerie. Sofie checked the area around the crime scene again without much hope. After the techs finished the report, cleaning mechs would come along and remove all trace of the murder. For now, while the crime scene techs analyzed the new evidence from their inspection of the passageway, the only disturbances came from the few residents who lived next to the site, three doors on each side. Most would be getting ready for their shifts, based on the schedule she'd found.

Rick and Amanda would be at work by now. Interviewing as a team got better results because it was harder to lie to or avoid answering two people.

She called Rick. "Ready to start the day?"

"I'm already halfway to the site," he said. "Are you there?"

"I'll wait for you. We've got maybe an hour to do the units in this passageway."

Ten minutes of pacing and trying to imagine how

someone would carry Oswald Sato's body to the dump site gave her no clues. The victim was a large man, but anyone could have hacked a mech to transport him. Although placing him on the top of one would require work. And there was no sign of rough handling. Maybe more than one person was involved. That wouldn't make anything easier.

"You want to split up?" Rick asked when he arrived. "We don't want people heading out for shift while we're in one unit listening to a bunch of gripes."

Sofie looked out to the main walkway. If someone did leave, they would have to pull them off work to question them. It might be interesting to see if that led to trouble.

"No. We'll start at the far end and work our way back. No dawdling."

The units were numbered 105573 through 105578. Each only big enough for two people and a few kids to occupy. No shift sharing either.

Sofie pressed the first panel to announce their presence. "Police. We need to talk to you."

Rick leaned his ear against the door. "Nothing happening inside."

"I guess we check." She typed in the override code and the door slid up, releasing the odor of dirty clothes and cheap fried food. "Anyone here?"

The question was just a matter of form. There was only one room. A bathroom section closed off the far corner. A tiny kitchen took the other opposite corner. Two bunks were raised and secured to the wall. An entertainment screen faced the beds. A table and two chairs filled the rest of the space.

"Maybe they're shacked up," Rick said. "No rule says you have to sleep at your own place."

Sofie made note of the names and let the door slide

down. "I hate tracking people down. Maybe Mitch knows them."

"Yeah, he really seemed like the nosy type." Rick moved to the next door.

One occupant answered them. Behind her the room was tidy and clean. She'd been doing a double the night in question. According to her, the other person assigned to the unit had an accident at work and spent the last day in the medical unit.

"We'll have to follow up on that," Sofie said. "Thanks for your time."

"You know where your neighbors are?" Rick asked, pointing to the first unit.

The woman wrinkled her nose. "Usually sleeping off drink in some flop or alley. They get loud when they're home. Haven't heard anything for a couple of days."

Sofie made a note for the recording. "And the others?" Gossip sometimes gave the best clues.

"The two near where the body was found are empty. The supervisor said someone will be moving in soon. I hope they're more respectful than those savages."

"And any of the other neighbors?" Rick asked in his charming voice. It worked with all kinds of people, not just ones he seduced. "You know a lot of what's going on around here."

"A family across from me. There was some kind of trouble a few days ago. Haven't seen much of them since. She might be home. I think he's taken off. The two kids are kind of young, but they're allowed to run wild."

"One more, right?" Rick said, pointing to the last unit. "It's definitely an interesting area."

"I think the guy is running prostitutes, and you cops don't do anything to keep my street decent. Men and women coming and going most of the day and night." She looked over at the door. "I guess even he needs to sleep. Maybe he's home."

"Thanks," Sofie said. "We don't want to make you late. If you think of anything, call either of us." She handed the card with their comm codes on it.

The woman tucked it into a pocket and closed her door.

Despite the information, Rick checked all the units. The two empty ones were dusty but ready for tenants. "Mitch might be running a scam," Rick said. "Not a great area, but better than some. Probably charging for the right to move in."

"Asking for too much, if these have been empty for a while." Sofie made a note to dig deeper into the supervisor. "We can ask when we track him down."

Rick laughed. "Because our powerful interrogation skills will override his need to keep it quiet?"

"If not, he would be lying to us and that gives us something to work with later." The family unit was also empty. Clear signs of occupancy and kids. Toys in the corner. Food on the table. "Out shopping?"

"Yeah, or working for the guy next door. We'll find her later. Ready for our pimp?"

"Is anyone ever ready to talk to that kind of asshole?" Sofie pressed the panel and identified herself and Rick.

The door slid up to reveal a man in his thirties. His hair was cut short enough to let his scalp show through. His clothes were basic off-duty overalls. He yawned and scratched his chest. "Yeah?"

Behind him the unit was cleanish. No real mess, but not well-kept. It also didn't contain any more than the usual two bunks, table, two chairs, and an entertainment screen. Not a place she'd expect to be used for paid sex.

"We're investigating the murder," Rick said. "Body found in the recess yesterday?"

"Yes. I didn't do it." He gave a little chuckle.

"Just gathering information," Rick said. "Did you see anything?"

"No, and I'm here most of the time. Funny thing, I didn't hear anything either. You'd think a murder would be noisy, right?"

But dumping a body wouldn't make much racket. "May I ask why you're home so much? I thought this was a shift-worker area."

"I got injured and can't do much hard labor. So I agreed to run this unit as a short. The empty bed is assigned to people who need a break between long shifts. And I'm the local Accept protector. People come to me for shelter in hard times."

So not a pimp. Being the protector didn't guarantee he wasn't their killer, but it was unlikely. People drawn to that religion tended toward passive resentment of their position in life. They didn't claim that life was unfair or push for better treatment, and they didn't evangelize.

"Thanks for your time," Sofie said, handing him the card. "And if any of your visitors have information, give them the details to call."

He took the card and looked at it. "I will, but my flock don't come here to be interrogated." He slid the door shut.

"So, no sound of conflict," Rick said. "More evidence that the body was dumped."

"Yes. And I have something more to tell you." Sofie passed on Nhu's message about the kids.

"How many?" he asked. She saw a flash of anger cross his face.

She gave him the number she'd uncovered. "Too many, right?"

He swore. "If we aren't investigating, that means someone is doing more than taking a few credits for looking the other way. Who's assigned to the cases?"

This hit Rick harder than Sofie expected. Nothing she knew about him explained the anger. Yes, it was appalling, but so much of life on the Mallet fit that description. "I didn't make a note, but it's not just one officer."

She noticed Rick's hands clenching into fists. Then he relaxed and she could almost hear him counting to ten. "Not our job, right? I'll look into it on my own time. After we solve our case and learn if any of them are linked to Sato."

She wouldn't tell him how to handle his own secrets. "Okay, maybe I'll help you with that. Right now, we need to find that mother next door and her children. I don't recognize the name from the reports, but I'm guessing not all get called in. And whatever is going on isn't taking a break while we investigate."

12

They found Mitch banging on a unit door a few passageways away.

"Give me five minutes," he said. "Got to make sure these ones are up and ready for work."

"No more than five," Sofie said.

"You can wait for me at the stim stand around the corner," he said. When they didn't walk away, he swore under his breath and returned to his task.

Sofie had no intention of letting him slip away on some pretense. She'd checked on the duty list for his job, hoping it would shed light on what he should know about his area. Nothing on there about waking people up for work. So either there was a side deal going where he got paid for fully-staffed shifts — possible — or he'd sold it as a service to the tenants — also possible. Or both, which was the most probable.

He banged on the last door, receiving a yelled response to do something that would likely cause him injury if he tried.

"Okay, now what can I help you with, officers?"

"We could use that stim-juice now," Rick said. "Wouldn't want to get in anyone's way standing here."

Mitch looked around the passageway and then turned to walk to the main corridor. "Sure. I don't have to babysit these layabouts all the way to the job."

There were a few stools and tiny tables welded to the floor around the stim stand. No one else was enjoying a morning jolt, so Sofie ordered the drinks and joined Mitch and Rick at the farthest cluster.

"Thanks, my turn next time," Rick said, reaching for his drink.

"One day, your 'next time' will coincide with everyone else's definition of the term." Sofie hitched her hip onto the seat of the stool they'd left for her. "We have some more questions." She placed her pad on the table between them, the recorder turned on.

"Whatever you need." Mitch concentrated on sipping his stim-juice. "This is a messy business. Every man's death is to be regretted, but an Elite? That causes complications and interruptions."

Really? Sofie didn't like his sanctimoniousness, but perhaps they could play on it. "We received a tip that kids are going missing," she said. "What do you know about it?"

He suppressed a choke on the stim-juice but not quick enough for Sofie to miss it. She checked Rick's reaction and saw his tell, a tiny smile at the corner of his mouth.

"Do you suspect me?" Mitch asked, sounding offended at the implication. "I assure you that I don't trade in children."

"We don't suspect anyone right now," Rick said. "Just looking for information."

"Why would I know anything about it?"

His role in the case had moved rapidly from a possible

tool to get information to an outright suspect. Sofie reached for her pad to make a note, letting Rick continue with the questions.

"You are the area supervisor. You know who lives here. I assume since you take it as your responsibility to make sure your residents are up and ready for work on time, you also know who isn't here."

He picked up his drink again. Sofie sat patiently, waiting for him to come up with the next lie. Rick was an expert at pushing until someone gave up trying to hide their secrets. It worked for the job, but some days he was a pain in the ass to be near if you had a secret and he wanted to know what it was.

"Do you expect us to believe you aren't observant enough to notice?" Rick pushed again. His voice was light in contrast to the words.

Mitch wiped his lips and then waved the suggestion off. "Of course not. And I know other sections have been plagued with this problem. But it's been going on for years. Why are you interested now?"

"Because a dead Elite was found in your section," Rick said. "Now we get to be interested in anything we think will solve the case."

Mitch closed his lips tight. Sofie waited for Rick to push him again, but Mitch sighed as though resigning an internal debate. "Of course. I understand how it is. What exactly do you need from me? I assure you I don't know much."

"How many children?" Rick asked. "Recently?"

"In my section, four. Others run off for a few days, but four children seem to be gone permanently."

"What are the family names, and their units?"

"I'd have to look it up," Mitch said.

"You don't know?" Sofie asked. "How is that possible?"

"I know the names," Mitch said. "But I have other details. I'm sure you want to know when they were last seen, the family situation, any friends who might know?"

"Yes, all that," Rick said, "but names will suffice right now."

"Two of the Zim kids, but that was a while back. And the Smitt boy Kal, a couple of weeks ago, and Bebee Lyman. She hasn't been seen for three days." He added the unit numbers. "Don't know who will be around if you plan to interview them."

"Did you report any of this?" Sofie asked.

"Not my job, or my business. I'm busy keeping the people calm."

"What does that mean?" Sofie asked.

Mitch stilled. He'd said something he, or someone else, wanted kept quiet. "Nothing. I have to deal with a few rowdy drunks is all."

"We'll follow up," Rick said. "Those details you promised better be sent in the next hour, or we'll come back. You won't like that."

Mitch tossed his cup into the recycler and stood. "Then I'll get on it."

Sofie didn't object. She checked the list she'd down-loaded from the database. "None of those names were reported."

"Let's see what he sends us," Rick said.

"He didn't mention those kids Nhu told us about," she said. "What constitutes 'permanently missing' around here?"

"Something we'll find out," Rick said. "I got a few errands. See you back at the office?"

"Sure." Sofie wanted to track down Deacon, the guy she'd given meds to yesterday. Maybe he had something that would help them. And she wanted to see if he was okay or if he'd felt an attack when the meds were supposed to be working.

She found him at the same corner. He looked sick still, but the meds weren't miracle workers.

"Officer," Deacon said. "A wonderful day."

"So, you feel better," she said. Now that she had the chance, she couldn't bring herself to ask about the effectiveness of the drugs. If he said they worked perfectly, it would mean her condition was worsening. She asked him what he knew about missing children instead.

"Always been happening," he said. "Though, come to think of it, there seem to be more incidents. You think it's related to the dead Elite?"

"No idea," she said. "You have my contact card?"

He patted his pocket. "Safe and sound."

"If you hear anything, reach out." She slipped him a few more meds.

"I do have something," he said. "It may be a coincidence."

She waited. If he was going to be an ongoing source, she wanted to set out the relationship as she expected it to continue. No time-wasting banter.

"It's not just kids," he said. "Too often the parents disappear shortly after. Look into that."

If it was related, Oswald definitely had a very powerful partner, or perhaps multiple. And that opened up a whole new avenue of motive.

13

"I thought Amanda was going to do all the grunt work," Rick said.

Sofie looked up from her pad. He was good at the research, but he hated it. To be fair, no one loved being tied to a desk during an investigation. Well, no one except Amanda, despite her initial objection. "It's what we have to do right now," she said. "Amanda can't do it all for you."

"I could be out poking into corners. Asking questions. Finding the actual kill site." He put his booted feet on the table and tipped his chair to balance on the back two legs, his pad resting on his thighs. He started flipping through whatever he'd pulled from the database.

"What corners?" Sofie asked. If he had some lead that would take her out of the office, she'd race him to the door.

"Is there someone to answer your questions?" Amanda asked. For once she seemed to be on Sofie's side. Perhaps teasing Rick was something they could unite on.

"Shut up," he said. "I'm thinking."

Sofie laughed and threw a balled-up printout at him. "You only have a few names to check," she said.

Amanda tapped her own pad. "I hate this part. When the case is so new you have nothing but rumors and gossip. And a dead body."

Sofie looked at the names on the list she'd pulled this morning. Missing kids but not the three names Mitch gave them. "One of the rumors is that it's been going on for ages."

Rick looked up. "Is this all of the missing Maintenance kids?"

Sofie double checked her search criteria. "No. Just the part near the body dump."

"I'll pull up the whole section," Amanda said. "You might have actually had a good idea."

Rick smirked and went back to his pad.

"Check on the whereabouts of the adults too," Sofie said. "At least we can poke into their corners and ask them questions."

"It'll be five minutes to collate and download," Amanda said. "The queue is busy, and I put in an order to analyze for patterns."

This should have priority.

"It should be easier to find the adults," Rick said. "They'll have work shifts. Kids might slip notice, but someone not on the job is going to stand out."

Sofie checked the time. Her meeting with June Sato was in an hour. The Second wouldn't be satisfied with rumors and gossip either. Until she had a reason to suspect anyone, Sofie wasn't going to hand over any names or clues. June Sato wouldn't be happy, but sharing information before an arrest was a sure way to screw a case.

"You think the Elites know anything?" she asked. "Their gossip will be different."

Amanda was standing at the wall, reviewing the information up there. "Are you saying you think they'll share? Or be honest?"

Why did she have to say it like she assumes I'm stupid? "No. But what they refuse to tell us will help too, right? And if they have a scapegoat in mind, it would be nice to know."

Amanda nodded. Before she could speak, her pad pinged. "That's the data."

She projected it onto one of the many clear patches of the wall.

"Holy shit," Rick said. "How did anyone miss this?"

Two lists scrolled up the wall. One, names of kids who were missing, and the other, names of parents who hadn't reported for their shifts. The first list kept scrolling after the second was done. Maybe twenty adults. More than three times as many kids as the first list she'd pulled.

"What time period?" Sofie asked.

"This year," Amanda said. "Just this year. Maintenance only."

Even if this wasn't related to their case, this could cause riots if anyone else put it together. Maintenance might be huge, but it wasn't possible anyone could miss this many kids disappearing — unless they were being paid to do so. Was that why the rumors about unrest were so common these days? The workers finally realizing the magnitude of the problem?

Rick took in a sharp breath. "Hard to believe it's not related, right? Something this big doesn't stay hidden without someone wielding power."

"Can you check the other sections?" Sofie asked. "All the other sections."

Amanda stopped the projection and put in the request. "We need privacy screening," she said. "This can't get out until we have more details, or some answers."

"I'll requisition it," Sofie said. "Until we have it, nothing gets projected again."

"We need it on our pads," Rick said. "Related or not, we're in Maintenance, maybe we can find some of them."

"There are no missing children in any other section," Amanda said quietly. "Not even closed cases. You think it's Oswald Sato?"

No wonder the section felt off, Sofie thought. No one could possibly know the total. But each section of Maintenance had too many to keep secret. No one cared enough to fight for them. No one thought the cops would do anything. "It's a motive if he's involved. That's going to bring way too many suspects to follow up on. Run the names we have against the lists."

"You think there are unreported names?" Amanda asked. "Of course there are. What was I thinking?"

They had three names from Mitch: Zim, Smitt, and Lyman.

"Zim is on here," Amanda said. "Mother reported. Smitt too. But that's all. So we could be looking at only two of every three incidents being reported."

"We can only work with what we have," Sofie said. "And some of the kids left on their own. Found work in a black market or ended up in the dark streets. But now we have a list of people to question, Rick."

"Yeah, and Mitch hasn't sent us his details like he promised," Rick said. "Amanda, can you send the list of area supervisors for the whole section?"

"You won't be able to talk to them all," she said. "Only one dead Elite."

"Still, the names will come in handy," Sofie said. "And we don't know where Sato was actually murdered."

"Yeah, we need that before we do anything else." Rick

tapped his pad. "It's got to be covered in blood. Hard to believe no one has found it by now. Aren't the mechs supposed to report anything unusual as they clean?"

Yes, Sofie thought, but if no one reads the report, no one follows up. "Amanda, find those reports." If she hadn't been panicked about getting an attack of the Fades, she'd have requested the information yesterday after the meeting with Llewelyn.

"I'll send you the most promising places as soon as I find them," she said. "You have your meeting with the Sato Second coming up."

"I know. What are the odds she has information for us?"

"More likely she has the name of someone the Satos want to take the blame," Amanda said. "Don't fall for it."

There she goes again making like I'm naive, Sofie thought. "Already thought of that."

"Allen, my office now." The captain's voice snapped from the comm. "Alone."

"Probably not to give you a bonus," Rick said.

Sofie slapped his arm. "Asshole. I guess it's as good a time as any to tell him we need the room locked down."

14

———

Captain Llewelyn pointed to the chair across from his. The office was disturbingly tidy. Usually covered in reports, empty cups, and occasionally the remnants of a meal going moldy, today the desk was clear. The screens showed a peaceful scene of some planet's mountains, and there was not a cup or plate in sight.

Sofie sat and waited. He didn't want a report, he wanted to vent, and it was her job to take whatever he thought he could pass on.

"I received a holovisit from one of the Satos this morning. The current front-runner for Pratham."

It explained the state of his office. "Did they have anything to help find the killer?"

"Too busy jockeying for position to do anything but annoy me."

This wasn't why he called her in. The holovisit must have been arranged at the last minute. She figured the usual mess of reports was piled in a desk drawer. Perhaps June Sato would explain when they met. "I can bring Rick and Amanda in if you need to give us orders." It was too hard to sit passively waiting for the captain to get around to telling her why she was in his office.

"You are in charge of the investigation. You pass on anything I tell you unless I say otherwise. This was always going to need handling, but I thought I picked the right detective. Did I make the first mistake of my career appointing you lead?"

Hardly that. He screwed up as often as anyone. "It's early and that means little progress. I can explain to the Sato family."

The captain held up a hand.

"Don't be stupid enough to invite them in," he said. "Look, you know as well as everyone here, if you don't get traction in the next two days, you're looking at a dead case. I don't want to tell the Sato family we can't find the killer. I've had requests for updates from five of the Prathams and two Seconds. I'm not planning on letting you piss off all the Elites before you solve the case. I also don't want to settle for whoever they decide is expendable to close the case."

"I'm meeting with June Sato shortly. Perhaps as the Second she knows why we're getting more pressure than expected."

"It's a freaking Pratham, Allen. None of the candidates can show anything but concern. They do that by making our lives harder. Not one of them cares about anything but the opportunity created by his death."

Sofie fought the urge roll her eyes. Her knee was jiggling so she forced her foot flat on the floor. Showing impatience wouldn't speed up the flow of information, but sitting and waiting for Llewelyn to get to the point was just wasting time she could be using to look for missing kids and the killer.

"I need to prepare for my meeting. Is there anything you want me to ask the Second?"

"No. I checked on your investigation."

Everything they pulled from records would be logged, and whatever they entered into the system would be open to him. Sofie didn't like the fact that the captain was monitoring them, but she understood the need. "Rick and I have some notes we haven't logged."

"I'm not concerned about that," he said. His voice was soft but she could hear the stress of not yelling in it. "Why are you pulling records of missing kids from all over Maintenance? What the fuck does that have to do with the death of Oswald Sato?"

Sofie took a breath. She'd been hoping to firm up or dismiss the connection before reporting it. He could tell her to drop it and still avoid responsibility if the kids turned out to be motive — or killers. It wasn't his usual approach. Captain Llewelyn let his detectives run their cases, offering his help but never acting unsolicited.

"Is someone feeding the Satos information?"

"Of course someone is," Llewelyn laughed. "You mean is it Rick or Amanda?"

Oddly enough, she trusted them to keep the details to the team. Amanda's ambition could take her across a line or two. Rick less so; he wasn't immune to an offer of enough money to retire on, though. But she'd seen their reactions to the numbers of kids on that list.

It wasn't her. Unless Llewelyn was a much better liar than she thought, it wasn't him. It didn't matter anyway. The truth was the police force, like every other part of the station, was riddled with moles.

"My team isn't the problem," she said. "It could be

anyone in records. Someone could have hacked into our systems." Not easily, but it was possible.

"Why are you looking at missing kids?"

"Your Sato visitor knew that?" If true, it was a whole new level of surveillance.

"Thank the universe, no. I'm going to ask one more time, and this time I need an answer. Why are you looking at missing kids?"

"Did you see the logs or the information?"

"Logs."

"We got a tip that more and more kids were going missing. I wondered if it might be a motive. Maybe Sato was into some kinky shit and a parent went after him for revenge. Maybe he found out that someone else was into kids and got killed to stop him talking about it. Then we looked into it." She pulled her pad out and showed the captain the list, setting it to scroll slowly.

"They are all still open cases?" Llewelyn's voice lost the anger.

"Amanda only asked for open cases."

"Only Maintenance?"

She felt for him. That aching need to find a way for this to be some kind of horrible accounting error. "Only this year. And only what got reported. The real number could be higher."

He straightened his back and flicked on his screen. "I'll put someone on this now."

"Give us some time to see if there's a connection," Sofie blurted out. The last thing she needed was to lose control of the findings. "Whatever is going on will probably slow down with our presence. Let us run with it for a couple of days."

He squinted at his blank screen, as if reading the list of names that she knew must be rolling through his mind.

"If the media finds out?" he asked, turning back to her. "Not that I'm afraid of them, but we'll need answers, and my gut is saying the minute a Sato finds out, it will hit the news. And then we'll be facing protests and strikes and violence from Maintenance. You know that will spread to Manufacturing before we can deal with it."

"Let's hope they don't. Look, how much worse is it that we didn't know or ignored the data? You can say we're investigating because we are. Rick and I will follow up on the names. Parents are going missing too. If one of them is the killer, it makes sense for them to hide. But there's nowhere to go."

Sofie was sure the killer was higher up in the Mallet hierarchy than the parents of missing kids. But giving Llewelyn an alternate theory might relieve some of the pressure he got from above.

15

Sofie left the captain's office, ducked into the case room to give Rick and Amanda an update, and then hurried to an empty conference nook to join June Sato's meeting space. As she settled herself in the empty chair to wait for the Second to appear, she tried to run the warnings through her mind and sort out what to share.

I forgot to ask for the privacy screening. The thought tore through her concentration. Not what she needed. She would just have to remember to ask Amanda to do it.

A flickering above the other chair caught her attention. In a few seconds, June Sato's hologram appeared to be sitting across from her. The woman's location must have been built to the same specifications as this one. None of the usual glitches indicated a screened background covering some other details.

"This will be short," June Sato said. Her smile glowed against her dark skin. Her hair was pulled back tightly. She wore black but it didn't look severe on her, just professional.

"Of course," Sofie said. "What do you want to know?"

The smile widened. "To the point, I appreciate that. You

are aware that the incident has created some competition within the family?"

Competition was a nice way to describe the all-out war to take the Pratham title. Sofie sent a little thanks to the universe for keeping it away from the functional parts of the station. "Yes. I hope the decision will be made soon. I'm sure it is disruptive for the family."

"Indeed. I expect to be informed if any of your investigative efforts come close to the candidates."

Sofie bit back her first reaction, which was to say the details would not be made available to the public until the murder was solved. While true, no one said no to an Elite. "So far we have no suspects. As I'm sure you know, this early on we are still gathering details. Some of what we discover will turn out to be completely unrelated." Perhaps that was true about the kids, but her gut didn't think so.

"Precisely. I do not wish to interfere with your job, Detective. Oswald was my friend as well as my Pratham. I want the killer found and brought to justice. No matter who they are."

"Then we are in agreement," Sofie said. "The sooner we gather and follow leads, the sooner justice can be applied."

June said nothing to that. She looked down at the desk. On her side of the holo, there would be notes and a screen and other normal office things.

"Is there something you wish to tell me?" Sofie asked. This woman probably knew everything about the family business. It was her job to keep life running smoothly for the Satos, regardless of how her efforts affected the rest of the station.

"If I knew who committed this vile act, don't you think I would have given you the name?"

Unusual for a Second to display emotion. Their jobs

relied on impartiality; showing emotion meant an allegiance to a side. But it might not be a side in the case. While the murder was Sofie's only focus, June Sato had the usual stresses of her job, and the fight for Pratham, and, if she told the truth, grief over a murdered friend.

"Sometimes people have knowledge they don't realize is important," Sofie said, keeping her tone neutral. "If we knew the victim's interests, it is possible we would find a lead there."

"I will not share family secrets," June said. "And despite our reputations, the Seconds are not always included in business activities. The only thing I know that might be of help is that Oswald was working with another Pratham to grow a business venture. He did not yet think it was worth including in the family ledgers."

Because it was something people would object to on the grounds of morality? Sofie stifled the laugh. The Elites wouldn't care about morality. They valued money and power.

"It is something we can add to our tasks," she said. "Were there any particular personal disagreements? Within the family? One of the current candidates, perhaps?"

The smile came back. "You think one of the successors became impatient? They would not dispose of him in such a public manner."

Not that they wouldn't kill him.

"I thank you for your time," Sofie said.

"Before you go, are you willing to tell me where your investigation is leading at the moment?"

That was the real focus of the meeting, although Sofie knew June had two goals. The first she had accomplished, putting the other Prathams under suspicion. Now the off-the-cuff question.

"The information we have at this time reveals several promising avenues, but nothing more than that."

The smile wavered a moment and then came back. "Thank you. If anything changes, I expect to hear it from you, not the local news outlets."

June ended the connection and Sofie was alone again. It had taken longer than she thought for the Elites to move beyond just putting pressure on the captain.

Sofie sent a note to Amanda about the privacy screening and the scraps of information June Sato had tossed her way. *I'm not sure how credible the tips are,* she added. She should join them in analyzing the names they'd found, but the thought of going back made her feel like she was hiding. The answers were in the Maintenance section. Not with Mitch, who was hiding something — more than one something — but with people like Deacon or the neighbors. Or the parents of those two kids Mitch told them about.

If she told them where she was going, Rick would take the opportunity to join her, leaving Amanda with the data. Two perspectives would be an asset when they found something in the case room. And she wanted to go solo.

She set a notification to send in an hour to let them know what she planned. Maybe that would be enough time to find a lead. Maybe it would be enough time for her to find the kill site. What burned in her gut was the thought that it was definitely enough time for more kids to disappear.

————

16

The body site was starting to feel familiar. Not a good thing; familiarity took away a detective's sharp observation skills. Sofie turned her back on the recess and closed her eyes. After a moment's reflection, she opened them and turned on the holo of Oswald Sato's body. The scene should look fresh to her now. And without Rick, she could turn the body as she wanted. The scene looked seamless, but it was a collection of smaller holos, each able to be examined separately.

She called up the list of items taken in as possible evidence and held it just out of her line of sight. First, she'd walk through the scene and think about what should be on the list, then she'd look at it. It was critical to investigate from her own observations rather than get trapped verifying what someone else had done.

Everything currently in the recess still showed through the projection, leaving her with a slight case of vertigo if she looked too closely.

No mech had cleaned the area. Good. It gave her a better chance of reading the evidence. The body sprawled on a diagonal. There were no blood smears or spatter, reinforcing the idea this was a dump site. She didn't relish searching the station for a bloody murder scene. Although Maintenance was the only section one would go unreported. Maintenance and possibly the Temporaries.

She stood at the entrance to the site. If he'd been dumped dead, he would have been upright and tipped onto the floor. Like the murderer placed him on a dolly and transported him. To stay upright on a dolly, he must have been strapped in, or in rigor.

She reached in, tapped the body and twisted her wrist to rotate it. No marks indicating he'd been tied onto anything. She checked the autopsy notes. Nothing on the body either. Lividity indicated he lay facedown for a time after death.

She typed a list of items she expected to be on the evidence list as she walked through the scene. Murder weapon? DNA? His possessions?

When she was ready, she checked the official list. No weapon, but who would transport that with the body? DNA from dozens of people — it was a garbage recess, so no surprise there. She was in for a lot of footwork checking each contact. Nothing unusual in his possessions, either in what they found, or what was missing.

Sofie noticed one of the techs had been enthusiastic enough to open the panels and collect evidence from the garbage tank. The only thing listed was a scrap of blue fabric caught inside the catch. The tech suggested it was a woman's scarf and had not been in the tank long. Unfortunately, long enough for the chemical fumes to degrade any organic material — no DNA.

It was time to look for the real murder site herself. A team of lower-rank officers had been dispatched, but Maintenance was a big place. With what she'd seen here, she could start at the equipment stores. Maybe luck would be on her side and a bloodstained dolly would be waiting for a cleaner with the murderer's name attached to a tag. The thought drew a laugh.

She headed out of the area toward the stores section.

"Detective." The voice belonged to Deacon. "Good to see you still on the job."

"Always," Sofie said. Deacon looked healthier than the first time she'd seen him and better than this morning. The pills were doing their job. The upside of the Fades, if you could call it that, was fast recovery. When you weren't suffering constant symptoms and attacks, your body healed. Now that he didn't look like he was waiting to be shoved out an airlock, her pity turned to fear. He must know she suffered too. One more person who could tell her secret.

"That body still not solved?" Deacon asked. "Sato guy, right?"

"The Pratham, yes," Sofie said. "Do you know anything about it? Or are you looking to gossip?" Suppressing his condition might have opened his memory, or made him as nosy as most healthy people. Or he could know something helpful and finally be willing to tell.

"Used to come here a lot," Deacon said. "In disguise, like. You only knew it was him if you looked close."

A new angle. Maybe the killer didn't know it was a Pratham until it was too late. "His body wasn't disguised."

"You know the Elites. Sometimes they think a fact is true because they want it to be and they miss the mark on a detail or two. He did a fair job on the disguise, but when you looked close, the boots were higher quality than the rest of the clothing, which was a bit worn. He walked like he had all the time in the universe, not like the rest of us."

So the outer clothing was missing. Another clue without a lead and a lot of material to misdirect the investigation.

"You know what he was doing down here?" Even a guess might be useful.

"Not for sure. Maybe looking for a bit of rough company. Maybe business. Never saw him meet anyone."

"Where did you see him most? Here?"

Deacon glanced at the corner leading to the dump site. "No. Mostly he was coming or going from the dark streets. That's why I thought it was a sex thing."

The dark streets were largely left to police themselves. Despite the name, there were few incidents in the area. The people who ran the gangs didn't like attention; a bloody murder of an Elite would bring attention in droves.

"That might help," she said. It wasn't a place she wanted to go alone, but the longer she waited the more time someone had to clean up enough to fool the techs.

"I got a question," Deacon said. "Not about the murder."

"I don't have any more meds," Sofie said. "You should be able to get them from a clinic now. You're healthy enough to work."

He nodded. "Don't have a shift yet. But I was wondering where you got the meds. Just in case, you know."

He'd need to work a few shifts before he qualified for decent clinics, but the supply she gave him was good enough to cover him. "Don't you have any left?"

"Yeah. But you know how the Fades work. I can't afford to miss a shift."

She was well aware of the fear of a sudden attack. She went to sleep with it and woke up with it. Only work kept the thought from her mind during the day. One attack could change everything Deacon had arranged to improve his life.

"What makes you think I don't get them from a clinic? As a public service."

"Yeah, like anyone cares about us down here. Why do you think people are so pissed?"

"What do you mean, 'pissed'?" she asked. If the rumors about unrest were true, it still ran underground, unless she was too focused on the case and missing the clues on the streets.

"All kinds of shit going down here. People missing, right? I got my shifts because someone didn't show up for a couple of days. It won't take much to blow the lid off."

"I'll keep my eyes open," she said. "Do you know who had the job before you?"

"Some guy. Went missing, I heard his kid is gone too. Maybe they got off-station. Maybe got recycled. I don't care. I got my job. No one goes looking for workers who don't show up for a few shifts."

It doesn't make sense. Workers need to be on the job and it's not like we can just fly new ones in. "I'll talk to my supplier about introducing you. No promises."

17

Getting into the equipment stores without a lot of arguing and negotiation meant bringing someone with the right authority. Sofie's badge tended to push people into a defensive stance. People wanted warrants to cover their asses. She wanted speed. That meant finding Mitch. As the supervisor, he would be in and out of stores all day.

And he was still hiding something. If a Pratham was prowling around here, he should know, and he hadn't mentioned it. If she had to choose between Mitch and Deacon as a source, it would be hard. Mitch might be better on the stand in a jury trial, if this went to a judge. But she wasn't worrying about court.

Today she trusted Deacon. Even if he had reason to lie to her, she was his source of meds. And he couldn't afford to have them cut off if he wasn't able to access legit medical help yet.

She tapped Mitch's contact information into her comm unit. No answer. If he had the unit with him, he'd know she was reaching out. No guarantee he'd answer. She debated calling in a look-for alert. If he was hiding, that could send him deeper.

Time to try her luck with the equipment stores manager. Maybe whoever they were, they'd cooperate.

As it turned out, the man in charge didn't put up much resistance.

"Any equipment returned in unusual states?" Sofie glanced into the bay while she asked. Rows and rows of equipment lined the floor.

"Hah, no such thing as a usual state down here, Officer."

"Detective," Sofie said automatically. "Any returned in the last couple of days that haven't been cleaned?"

"No," he said. "Can't afford equipment lying idle. Everything gets cleaned and repaired within two hours. Ready to go back out."

There would be no evidence left. Cleaning was basically a dip in an acid bath and a spray of new paint. "Anything missing?"

"We don't do inventory every day, Detective. Could be, but who's going to keep a dolly or a forklift? They got trackers."

Really? That might prove useful. "Does everyone know about the trackers?"

The man rubbed his chin, leaving a smudge of black grease in the stubble. "Can't say who might know. It's not exactly a secret, but we don't publish it. You think someone stole one?"

Sofie didn't want to give this man any more details than necessary. Gossip could kill an investigation faster than anything else. Most people drew their secrets closer, and others deluged the department with tips hoping for a reward.

"Yes," she said. "How do we find out if all the equipment is accounted for?"

"Anything specific?"

"Just any discrepancies will be fine."

"Takes a few steps. We run the tracker records and then go count the units. If you can tell me what kind you're looking for, it will be faster."

Or I can get our tech team to do it. Sofie rejected the idea as soon as it rose to mind. The police team would need to work with this man, and he could make things hard if he felt slighted.

"When was the last inventory?" Maybe she didn't need a new one.

"Ten days ago," the man said. He frowned at her and then sighed. "Look, I get it, Detective. You don't know if you can trust me. You can, but I know that doesn't help. If you can't tell me what you need, give me some dates. I can try matching records."

"Three days ago to now. How long before you can tell me?"

"It's going to be a day," he said. "I'll send you a list of the people who requisitioned equipment, those who still have it, and what kind of equipment it was. That good enough?"

Not even remotely. "As fast as you can." At least this guy would give her something usable and not the list of items that had nothing to do with her needs that the records department would produce.

"That list I can send you within the hour. It's still going to take a day, maybe more, to find out if anything is missing."

Rushing him won't help. Sofie gave him her contact card and turned to leave. The dark streets were her next destination. Then back to the office.

"Detective," the man called to her. "There's something else before you get the inventory. I don't want you blaming me, right?"

"What is it?"

"If something is missing, and the person knows about the tracker, they can remove it."

"Okay. Let's hope that's not the case," she said. He was still holding something back. "What else?"

"Look, this is something the boss wouldn't like getting out, right? We're fixing it, but..." He took a deep breath. "The tracker inventory got wiped. A few cycles ago. We're rebuilding it, but if the one you need is gone, we won't be able to find it."

A few cycles meant a hundred or more days. "Why is it taking so long?"

"Being done on the quiet."

Why is everything so hard?

"Do you know why the records were erased?"

"Probably that power blip, remember?"

Sofie couldn't forget the nanosecond when the Mallet went dark. Thankfully, it was over before anyone could act on the instant panic. She'd held her breath for a while, along with every other person on the station, waiting for it to happen again. Within a couple of days, everyone went back to normal. "Any chance it was done on purpose?"

"The blip? Unlikely." There were plenty of people who could hack or bribe their way into the systems, but no resident of the Mallet would risk annihilation. "The records wipe? No idea."

"Okay, do your best," she said.

The dark streets were a cluster of corridors and open squares in the far corner of Maintenance, near the Temporaries section. The shift change was in ten minutes and the walkways would be crowded before Sofie could make it. If she took her time, maybe she'd find the missing Mitch. And get a stim-juice. And think.

Her route took her around the shopping squares. She grabbed her stim-juice from the first stand. People bustled around her, not paying any attention to the cop on the street. Two groups of men clustered at the corner casting glances her way.

One group was busy preaching the latest crap from the Came Befores. They usually handed out their brochures quietly. Lately something was stirring them up into a frenzy of converting people. Sofie didn't have much time for any of the religions on the station, but she did worry when behaviors changed. At least none of the other religions were stirring up their congregations, as far as she could see.

The second group of men dispersed while she watched. Was this normal behavior that seemed more sinister because of the rumors, or was it the beginning of something that would spiral out of control? She scanned the square again, not seeing anything unexpected, but made a mental note to keep alert for signs.

Sofie drank down the last of her stim-juice and tossed the container into the recycler. Time to move.

She strode across the square and entered the first passageway. Inside it was quiet. A few cross streets held residences. At the entrance to one was an elevator to take kids to the school level.

Doors rolled up in the residences as she passed. People preparing to head in for their shifts. A shout made her turn her head. Only a loud farewell, but a figure slipped into the shadows behind her.

She continued in the direction of the dark streets, but now she was on alert. The figure looked very much like one of the Came Before evangelists. Maybe going home, maybe not.

At the next corner she glanced back. Yep, the same person ducked around the corner. Sofie scanned ahead. The dark streets were visible as a void in the dimness about ten intersections away. There was a recess ahead. She slipped inside and waited.

Ten minutes went by and no one came looking. She was just being paranoid.

Her fingers started tingling as she stepped onto the walkway. *Fuck!* Sofie pulled out a couple of meds and dry swallowed them.

She couldn't quite get rid of the feeling she was being watched. Paranoia wasn't a symptom of the Fades, but it was one of the side effects of her job. She needed to get to Dr. Bindes before trying to get any information from the residents of the dark streets.

18

The Open Pit was just on the other side of the void ahead. A straight path through would take her to the Temporaries, but a left-hand turn halfway through would dump her into Maintenance about five minutes from the Open Pit. If she took the safer path through Maintenance, it would take three times as long to wind through the maze of residential passages.

The tingling subsided in her fingers. She checked her stunner. Fully charged. The people running the dark streets might not want trouble, but they had ways of dealing with unwanted guests. She might not be in for a full-on attack of her condition, but the onset left her feeling vulnerable and jumpy. If she was feeling normal, Sofie wouldn't chance entering the dark streets alone. She'd take the longer route. Now, in a hurry to see Bindes and afraid she might react badly to even the slightest threat, she needed the reassurance her weapon gave.

One more quick look around before she stepped out and pushed through the crowd toward the entrance to the dark streets. The crowd might slow her, but it also gave her cover.

The entrance looked less like a deep black void than it did from a distance. It wasn't exactly unlit, but the lighting was dim and the occasional flash and buzz of a fixture in need of repair gave the feeling of long abandonment.

The flow of people heading for their shifts bent a little to avoid proximity with her. Like they were afraid she would grab an arm and drag them into a life of misery — or more misery.

Sofie strode into the street, keeping to the center of the walkway. A few men and women idled inside residences, leaning against unit walls and watching every movement on the streets through the windows. She smelled alcohol in the air, at once stale and ripe with harsh flavoring, and the ever-present burnt grease and fog of human odor.

She kept walking, careful to appear uninterested in the activities she would have arrested anyone for outside this area.

One of the men peeled away from the group and stood in front of her. Sofie stopped. The right play was to confront him, not engage in a dance of dodging and apologizing. This was a gatekeeper and his life probably depended on making sure troublemakers were kept out.

"You take a wrong turn, Detective?"

His relaxed stance didn't fool Sofie. There was probably a stunner aimed at her from the shadows. He only needed to signal, and her body would disappear in a trash receptacle. And she'd forgotten to let Rick know she was headed here.

"Just passing through this time." She kept her gaze on his face, resisting the urge to scan him for weapons. *Keep things loose.* He should let her through, and send a message to whoever was ahead to hide the worst crimes in progress. Stopping Sofie could bring her back with reinforcements.

"Not a frequent choice for shortcuts. You sure you ain't here for business? Yours or ours?"

"Like I said, just on my way through. No plans to cause trouble."

He nodded slowly like he was considering his options. "Where you headed?"

All her training told Sofie to say it was none of his business. That cops didn't answer to scum. She was thankful for her ability to keep her emotions off her face. She waited to answer so he would think she was assessing him. "The Open Pit. Going through saves me time I don't have to waste."

He looked over to his group, who'd moved out of the shadows. Sofie braced herself. She could stun a couple of them, but the odds were against her in numbers, and desperation.

One of the women blinked slowly twice.

He turned back to her. "Don't cause trouble, you get none back."

He moved aside with a sarcastic bow and sweep of his arm, and Sofie stepped past him.

The area was set out as a rough circle of units. Two major walkways split it into four sections, each with its own lieutenant reporting to the head of the area. Each section offered all the pleasure, pain, and oblivion a person could afford. Not many visitors had the credits, so favors and trade were the economy.

Sofie would turn left at the intersection and keep walking until she was out. It wasn't the first time she'd been here, and it wouldn't be the last. Each time she wished she could keep her eyes focused on her feet and not notice the utter despair. But looking at her feet was a submissive position, and she couldn't display weakness. So, she stared ahead to where the intersection would be and tried to filter out the rest.

The rest was impossible to completely ignore. No dead bodies. They would be cleared to waste disposal, some after their bodies had been used for ugly purposes. But women and men were propped up in corners, oblivious to their surroundings. The sound of violence down a cross alley. The smell of blood adding a sharp tang to the usual stink. The muttered pleas for money, or offers of it for her compliance, or more if she fought back.

Sofie reminded herself to breathe.

The intersection was only two streets away. Her surroundings wouldn't get better, but turning the corner was a halfway point. Right now, she was going deeper into the dark streets. After the turn she would be leaving. She wouldn't come back here without Rick, ever.

It wasn't a big improvement, but as soon as she turned the corner, Sofie did feel her muscles relax a tiny bit. She sped up and then checked herself. Running for the exit wasn't a good look. She started counting the seconds in her head. Five minutes and she would be out. Twenty cross streets.

Down the next cross street something darted from one shadow to another. Sofie stopped. Was she being tracked to make sure she left? Probably. She continued on.

She could see the light of the normal Maintenance area ahead. Three more cross streets. Similar clusters of guards waited to stop trouble coming in. No one was looking her way, but they knew she was coming. They'd report in as soon as she stepped past the boundary.

A figure stepped out of the shadows beside her and wrapped an arm around her neck, dragging Sofie into the empty, dark street before she could call out.

19

S ofie jerked her body away from her attacker but the pressure on her neck kept her from fighting hard. One wrong move and she'd be dead. If this was what safe passage looked like, the boss of the dark streets was losing control.

"Stop fighting me, little girl." A man's voice, raspy and deep, the heat of his breath in her ear.

She twitched her hand towards her hip pocket. Her weapon was trapped between their two bodies, but she had a blade.

The man slid his free hand to stop her.

She bent her knee to kick back into his leg, but he leaned forward and unbalanced her, forcing Sofie to plant both feet to stay upright.

His hand pulled out her blade. "Nice little toy." He tossed it behind him. "Only you getting hurt today."

Sofie tucked her chin and then dropped onto one knee, the move forcing him to loosen his hold enough long enough for her to take a breath.

He tried to lean back, but Sofie twisted to face him. Blue

eyes stared back at her, his face covered below by a black scarf and above by a tight-fitting cap.

"You ready to pay for attacking a cop under safe passage?" She grabbed her stunner and pushed it into his chest.

"Nice try," he said. "You stop looking for that killer and leave the families alone."

She fired the stunner and got a grunt in response. That should have knocked him to the floor.

"Damper jacket." He reached between them and forced the stunner from her hand.

"Who killed the Pratham?" She figured it was worth a try. "You?"

"No. Someone beat me to it. You know what he was doing?"

If she could keep him talking, maybe he'd forget to hold her so tight. All her efforts so far had only gained her a look at his eyes and the ability to talk. "Enlighten me."

"No chance. You look into him, but leave the justice to us."

"Who is us?"

He grabbed her wrist and twisted. Sofie had no choice but to turn away and go to her knees to avoid a bad break. Now he thought he held the power, but Sofie could see her stunner. Just out of reach. He might have chest armor, but a shot to his ankle would bring him down.

"Victims." He bent forward to whisper in her ear again. "Not just missing kids."

Sofie pushed the pain to the back of her mind. She twisted a fraction more and her fingertips touched the handle of her stunner. "We know about the kids," she said, letting the agony she felt carry into her words. "Lots. Missing all over Maintenance."

"Here too," he said.

There are kids here? Of course, the boss of the dark streets caters to all tastes.

She lunged for her stunner, pulling him with her.

He grunted and yanked on her arm, but that only helped her wrench her body around. She jammed her stunner against his ankle and pressed the trigger. He grunted, arched away, and fell to the floor.

Her hands were shaking. Too close. Some of the charge backwashed into her body, and that could trigger an attack of the Fades. Not enough to stun, but enough to slow her down. She had to move because the jolt would not keep her attacker down for long. She needed answers. Anywhere else, she would arrest him, but not here, not now. Dragging a resident of the dark streets out to the cells would not be easy, and probably not worth the effort.

She struggled to stand, then moved to where he was moaning in the dirt.

"Now you get to tell me what I want to hear." She picked up her blade and moved to his side. Wires showed at the seam of his jacket. She kept her eyes on him as she cut them. No more damping armor.

"Not talking," he slurred.

"Here's the thing," she said. "We're in the dark streets. Alone, I'm kind of useless as a cop. But I don't have to be one. A body down here? No one will come to investigate."

"Not talking," he said, a little clearer this time.

Sofie heard someone charging toward them. She wouldn't survive if he had reinforcements. "How many kids are missing from here?"

Three of the gatekeepers burst around the corner, illegal weapons raised. "Get out," the first man yelled.

Her attacker pushed himself to his knees and then stood. He shoved Sofie to the wall and ran.

"Stop him," she said.

Two of the gatekeepers slipped away. The third turned to her.

"No. You may have permission to pass through, but we take care of our own."

Her rescuer stood aside and pointed to the Maintenance streets.

"And if I come back?" She couldn't just walk away like a civilian. "With friends?"

He laughed and pointed again.

She strode out like nothing had happened. But something had. Not just the attack. The realization that someone was willing to take that much of a risk to divert the investigation. And her own words. A dead body in the dark streets wouldn't attract much notice. And no one would have a reason to move it or any of the valuables with it. In fact, they wouldn't have found the body at all. This case would be about a missing Pratham, not a dead one.

The adrenalin wore off as she moved away from the danger. Her wrist throbbed and she couldn't bend it. And her cheek burned. She'd picked up a cut on that filthy floor, but no tingles or tremors, so no imminent attack.

20

The Open Pit was crowded. Too many eyes on her injuries for Sofie's comfort, but it couldn't be helped. The closest legitimate clinic was still ten minutes away.

Bindes was huddled over his drink in the far corner, no current patient and no one sitting close waiting for his attention. The side wall had frames attached for booths. She had no intention of asking if the renovations were approved.

She ignored the bartender's offer of a drink and marched to Bindes like she wasn't scraped, swollen, and bleeding.

"We need to talk," Sofie said to pull his attention from the half-empty beaker. "Now. In private."

He looked up. "Shit. More than talk. What happened?"

Sofie didn't answer. She'd never needed his help beyond the meds, but she knew he operated an illegal clinic somewhere in here. Until he took her there, she would keep silent.

Bindes pushed himself up and tipped his head to a door in the shadows behind him. Sofie gestured for him to lead the way. She wanted to turn and see who was taking notice, but that could signal there was something to see. And she could go to the legitimate clinic when they were done if he couldn't help her with the injuries. Not to report an attack, just an accident.

When the door closed behind her, Sofie leaned against it to slow any attempt at entry until she was done.

"Let me see the damage," Bindes said as he pulled dressings from cupboards. "What happened?"

Sofie put her hand behind her back, wincing at the increased throbbing. "No need. I want to know what the hell is up with the meds."

He sat on the only chair in the tiny room. There was a desk, a monitor, and a narrow examination bed. In here he could perform minor operations. Nice setup. "What do you mean? They're the same supply as always."

"They aren't lasting long enough," she said.

He tilted his head, then took a penlight from a pocket. "Like I said, meds are from the same supplier as always. You know the condition is progressive."

She'd been silencing that fear since the first surprise symptoms. "Shouldn't I feel something else? I'm not tired. I still have my appetite."

He stepped closer and shone the light in her right eye. "Look up."

Sofie did as he asked. She wanted to tell him she didn't need an examination, but Bindes was still a good doctor. He wouldn't offer an opinion without some tests.

He flicked the penlight to her other eye. "Look down. Mmm."

"You know that sound is really annoying."

He put the light away. "Yes, that's why we do it. Tell me what happened."

She described the assault in the dark streets. Not the conversation, but the physical part.

"And how many doses have you taken?"

"Three. Should have only been one."

He slowly nodded. "Let me see the meds."

Sofie handed them to him. "They look the same."

"There are more than three doses missing," he said. "Memory going?"

"I gave some to a man in Maintenance. He was in a bad way. Can I send him to you?" She explained Deacon's problems.

"Yes. So, you aren't overmedicating. Stress? It can heighten the symptoms."

She should have known this wasn't going to be fast. "High-profile investigation. Frustrating, but no more stressful than any other."

He handed back the meds. "Don't give any more away. You need this supply, and you aren't a doctor."

Her hand was now so swollen she could feel the throbbing in her whole arm. Her face was stiffening from the abrasion too. She let him examine the wounds.

"Would you normally miss the clues leading to this kind of assault?" Bindes asked as he cleaned the wounds.

His actions stung enough that Sofie needed to take a breath before she answered. "Not usually alone in that place."

"You're making some bad decisions." He applied a mist of painkiller to her face, then a temporary skin to promote healing. "This is going to hurt, but not for long." He pressed a hypo syringe to her swollen hand.

Pain roared through Sofie from her fingertips to the toes on her opposite foot. She didn't have time to scream before it faded. The aftermath left her cold and sweating. "I need a bowl — now!"

He passed her a cardboard vessel and waited until she'd emptied her stomach. "Believe me, that's the easiest way to deal with your hand." He passed a wet towel to her.

Sofie wiped the sweat away from her face and tried to spit out the last of the foul taste. "I guess I should thank you," she said weakly.

"You should, but most don't. You should heal fast. No infection but I added a prophylactic just in case. Now, I want you to listen to me."

"I don't need a lecture, thanks. I want to know what's going on with the meds."

"I don't care what you want." He turned away and disposed of the mess. Then he handed her a glass of mint-smelling water. "Drink this. First, I'll look into the supplier. I think there might be a problem, but it doesn't mean your condition isn't gaining ground."

"I can't do anything about that," she said. The drink cleared the last of the bile from her throat. "Let me know what you find out." She stepped away from the door.

"I think you got that beating because of the Fades. You aren't fully alert. Whether it's worry about what's going on in your body or it's more symptoms, I can't be sure. But you wouldn't normally have missed the clues."

The fact that he was right didn't make the words easier to hear. "I have a big case. I can't step away right now."

"You should have the operation. If not in a legit place, then let me arrange it. Three, maybe four down days. Then you'll be fine."

Doing it off the books would solve her job problems. "I said I can't take any time off."

"At some point the choice won't be yours." He held up

his hands palms out. "I don't want to argue. You know my position and you know the risks."

"Fine, maybe when this case is done." She had the days to take the leave. And most cops spent time off in the Temporaries section where things were more carefree. So going off-line wouldn't raise too many questions.

"Let me know so I can set it up. I need to get back to my other patients. The swelling will go down in the next couple of hours. The temp skin will dissolve in a few days."

His words poked at something in Sofie's detective mind. *Other patients.* Like he ran a real clinic. "Do you treat anyone in the dark streets?"

"The bosses call me in there occasionally. A few of the workers make it here every couple of days. I'm not telling you who, Detective."

Sofie pressed the door sensor to keep it locked. "Not what I wanted. You hear any rumors about kids missing? Parents?"

"Yes, and that's all I can tell you."

She didn't have the energy to push harder. Bindes wasn't a suspect anyway. He cared about people too much to be involved in stealing kids.

21

"What might be happening with the meds?" Sofie asked Bindes, hoping he'd have some answers for at least one of her problems.

He opened a cupboard. Inside was a safe. She only saw the far side of the door and not how he opened it. Smart. None of his patients would have a clue how to start stealing meds.

A soft female voice welcomed Bindes to the contents.

"If it's the meds, it won't just be for the Fades." He pulled out a handful of vials and bottles. "If you have the operation, it won't be a problem."

"Not for me," she said. "But you have more patients with the condition. And they might not think to ask questions."

He arranged the containers on the table so she could see the labels. "If something is wrong, it's not because of me."

No motive for cheating his free patients. They had nowhere else to go, and he couldn't sell what he appropriated to buy more of his personal vice. VR was a highly addictive drug that took you to a better reality, but the dose needed never changed and the cost was minimal.

The dealers had plenty of volume and a need to keep their business low-key. Sofie always thought Bindes's work in here was some kind of penance or karma balancing for the fact that he had no intention of dealing with his addiction.

"I didn't think that. But you are the end of that supply chain. Between the lab and the patient there are a lot of stops."

He stopped arranging the bottles and vials. "All well within the expiry dates. The manufacturing seals are authentic."

It didn't matter. There was something wrong with the meds or there was something wrong with her, and Sofie wasn't ready to accept her fate. "All those things can be faked. You know that. Someone could be selling meds to people off-station, or keeping the initial ingredients back to make a more profitable street drug. Or maybe some crazy purity believer is trying to kill off anyone who needs help."

He sat back in the chair and stared at his inventory. Sofie waited while he thought about the problem. He was a good doctor, not just a VR junkie. He ran a legitimate clinic part-time; medicine was one of the few castes allowed to retire before their bodies broke down. And he might want her to take the surgery but wouldn't be stubborn enough to ignore her concerns. With his knowledge, he could probably rattle off another dozen motives for undermining confidence in the system.

"I know the suppliers. If you hadn't mentioned the problem, I wouldn't question their loyalty," he said. He snapped his gaze to Sofie, suddenly back in the real world. "There's one way we can determine the cause. I need to examine you. Determine the state of your condition. It's been a long time since I checked anyway."

"I don't have time." He could do a little investigation of his supply chain first.

"Ten minutes. Results will take an hour, but you don't have to wait around."

She couldn't avoid the procedure altogether, but each time he tested her she was tied up in knots waiting for him to confirm the worst. But he was right. If the Fades were progressing, it was better to know. When she finally had the procedure, she needed to be strong to recuperate.

"Fine." Sofie sat on the bed and waited for the probes into her reaction times and pokes of machinery extracting her bodily fluids. "Let's get this done."

It took less than the ten minutes he promised, but she was drained. Mostly the result of the adrenalin from the fight, but still a problem since she had to go back to the case room where someone could notice. She didn't want to report the attack and leave herself open to an official medical examination.

"I'll send you the results when I have them," Bindes said. "Same private code?"

"Yes. Can I get a stim?" It would keep her awake for hours, and the case was still waiting for her.

He handed her one pill. "I don't know what this will do given our questions about the Fades. It's mild. Take it with food. You can't take anything to help you sleep. Exercise or tea or meditation, that's all I will agree to."

She'd fall asleep on her feet if she didn't take it. Stim-juice wouldn't help enough to keep her going. "Promise. I'll pick up a sandwich on the way to my next stop."

He double checked all the vials of her blood and other fluids. "Okay, take it as easy as you can. Try to have someone with you for the next couple of hours. Even if the tests come back negative, you are still recovering from the assault."

Good advice that she was going to ignore. Rick would know something was wrong as soon as he looked at her. She'd go back to the office when she could face people without looking exhausted. And she'd have her results in an hour. One worry dealt with would help.

"And think about the operation." He stepped past her to open the door.

"I will as soon as I solve this case." She stepped into the hallway. "And you should start your investigation while you wait for the tests."

"I have other patients," he said. Taking a glance to make sure no one was close, he added, "Let's wait for the results. You look fine to me, but the Fades are tricky, and I can't risk my supplier stepping away because I'm asking questions."

Sofie left and strode through the Open Pit to the walkway outside. She checked her comm. Nothing from Rick or Amanda. She still had time to ask some questions. This time she'd take the long way round.

Talking with Bindes had eased her fears enough for her to realize the boss of the dark streets would have more reasons to move Oswald's body than just to hide the crime. Her mind was focusing better with the meds. If Oswald died in the dark streets, his body would make a good message to the boss's enemies: No one is too powerful to be dealt with; even Elites are vulnerable to their weaknesses.

The thought of going back set her bruises throbbing with pain. Later she'd come back with a handful of officers to search the dark streets for the real murder site.

22

Waiting for information made Sofie itch for action. Another reason to stay on the street; back in the case room, she'd end up looking at long lists of data for a crumb of a lead. The other thing prickling in the back of her mind was that one of their requests for information might just hold the clue that solved the case — or made sense of something.

She bought a roast sim-beef on rye at the first stand she found. Taking a stool at an empty table, she swallowed the stim and then took a bite of her sandwich.

She sent a query to Amanda. *Any news from the mech cleaner report?*

Nothing yet. No report from your area supervisor and nothing from the equipment inventory before you ask.

She could track down Mitch and force him to comply. He was an oily bastard. Seemingly willing to help, but never following through. And the mech reports shouldn't be taking that long. Unless the murder was committed in the one place no mech entered: the dark streets. A bloody alley in that section wouldn't be unusual.

She thanked Amanda, tossed her meal wrapper in a recycler, and headed back to Mitch's section.

He was nowhere to be found. If he was deliberately avoiding her, it was a matter of checking his schedule in the supervisor database. If he was missing, then the case could end up as a multiple murder investigation. Officially checking on his shift and whereabouts would cause him some aggravation with his superiors. Maybe he'd learn a lesson about dodging the authorities.

Sofie couldn't help but feel a little joy at the idea of Mitch getting a reprimand. She logged into the database and found he was supposed to be on shift. But no one tracked the supervisors, and databases didn't engage in conversations. All she knew was what he was supposed to be doing, and how to contact his immediate manager. Thank goodness for layers of bureaucracy. She entered the contact information and left a message for Mitch's manager to call her back.

Without Mitch to interrogate, Sofie had no excuse to stay away from the office. Unless she could come up with something, she'd be within range of the captain's interference. He wouldn't call her in from the field, but he would happily drag her into his office if she was in sight.

They needed to make progress. It had only been a day and a half since the body was found, but the case wasn't moving forward, and everything that looked promising just led to more nothing. Another couple of days like this and the crime would go unsolved. Her career would be sidelined to records management, the Elite families would send some innocent patsy to prison, and if people protested, they'd lock down the station.

Sofie looked around and found herself near the body dump site. She'd been walking while she thought, not so dangerous in this section of the Mallet but still foolish. She forced a positive thought through the bleakness. No, they didn't have any concrete clues, but they did have something. Mitch was probably hiding a little side-corruption, if not knowledge of the crime.

Kids were missing. She could follow up on that. At best link it to Oswald, at worst prove it wasn't related. She checked her pad and found the list of names. Parents who'd made the reports on missing kids. Zim, Smitt, and Lyman. She called Amanda and got a few more names.

"I'll be back after I finish interviewing."

"We've got a few messages. One from the Sato Second," Amanda said.

If she wasn't offering the contents of the message, there was a reason. Amanda was giving Sofie an option. Respond now or wait.

"I'll check them," Sofie said, careful not to say when.

"Hey, I've done my job." Amanda cut off the call.

Sofie sorted the names by proximity to her location. Seven interviews. Could take hours, or only long enough to leave a message depending who was on shift. She reordered them in a path that would end close to the office. The first name was Smitt. She and Rick already tried to speak to the mother, but no one had been in the unit. Maybe she'd have better luck now, when a different shift would be on the line.

She pressed the button and waited for a response. When no one answered, she pressed the comm and said, "Police. I will override the lock in one minute."

The door slid up immediately. A woman stood in the space, holding a hand out to stop a wandering toddler. She looked worn, like most of the occupants of the Maintenance area. Dark hair, pale skin, and too thin to be healthy. "Sorry, takes a minute to settle them so I can open the unit."

Behind her, Sofie could see three other children of various ages. She checked to make sure she was talking to Mrs. Smitt and then said, "We had a report that your children haven't been seen for a few days, are they missing?"

"You can see them," the woman said, tipping her head back to the room. "All accounted for."

"May I come in, so your neighbors don't hear our conversation?" Sofie didn't want to go in. Too many runny noses and sticky little fingers — and the slight odor of urine. Privacy would help if she had to get hard-nosed, though.

Mrs. Smitt glanced at the unit door across the way. "So she told you? She should worry about her own life. Not tell me how to raise my kids."

No invitation to enter, and Sofie didn't think forcing the issue would be a good idea. Pressure tended to close doors, not encourage confidences. "I can't confirm who made the report. I see four children, the report stated two?"

"I look after a couple of kids for a friend. No law against that?"

The neighbor said the two kids were too young to be running around. The children inside the unit definitely fit the description. "Were your children absent for an extended period?"

The woman picked up the toddler and propped him on her hip. "They went to find their father. He took off, but I guess they heard him talking to the bitch he left me for. He sent them back."

Sofie made a few notes, took the names of the children, and promised to close the case. Time to move on to the next name.

"You shouldn't be poking around in family problems," Mrs. Smitt said before Sofie took a step away. "You should find out who was banging around here a couple of nights ago. Woke my kids. I didn't get them back to sleep for hours."

Why was this news? No other neighbor reported noise. "The night the body was found?"

"Yeah. Most of the street was on shift, or in a bar. I heard a bang and then someone swearing. Then nothing. These units need an upgrade. Shouldn't have to hear what goes on out here."

Sofie took every detail the woman could remember, gave her a contact card in case she remembered anything else, and left her with an assurance she'd report the sorry state of the units.

She stopped at a stim-juice stall and filed her report with Amanda, asking her to follow up on all the data they were still missing. A metal dolly handled by an amateur could bang into a wall and Sato's body would have made a thump when it was dumped.

On her way back to the case room, Sofie visited the units on her list. An investigation could go wrong if the detective hopped around from lead to lead. Lesson number one, close off the loose ends.

Two more families, Ali and Madrona, introduced her to the kids who had returned and were working through their punishment for running away. The Van Brut and Surinat kids were supposedly at school. Amanda or a uniformed officer could check on that information. No one was home at either the Zim or Lyman units. Sofie tried to see this as progress. A happy ending for a family meant fewer children in peril. But none of this would break her case. And running around trying to track down people who were probably fine wasn't going to find the killer.

23

"You need to check your messages," Amanda said without looking up from her screen as Sofie entered the room.

"Who's been calling?" Sofie didn't plan to sit in the office, or in some meeting space wasting time. "Any tips we can use?"

"The usual hundreds of useless, time-wasting nonsense calls." Rick moved past her and put his pad on the table. When he turned around to face her, he winced.

"It's nothing," she said, knowing the temporary skin covered the worst of it.

He glanced at Amanda as if looking for support to argue with her, but Amanda gave him a tiny headshake. He took the hint and continued with his griping. "I swear if I have to hear another lie about some lover, husband, rival, or annoying boss killing an Elite, I'm going to start arresting people for being assholes. So, no real tips, and it feels like everyone has been calling."

Sofie sympathized. "Eventually, that will be against the

law, but I doubt the punishment will be death. Who do I need to call first?"

Amanda looked up from her screen. "June Sato. You'd know that if you looked at the list."

"What's got you in a mood?" Rick asked. "You've been sitting here in comfort. We've mostly been out in the stink of Maintenance."

"No one is responding to my requests," Amanda said. "How am I supposed to find answers without input?"

Sofie tuned out the bickering. It wasn't serious and would fade soon. The list of messages was short. June Sato and two from the equipment manager. Rick had taken all the tips. No wonder he was fed up.

She called the equipment manager only to leave a message of her own that he didn't need to wait for her, either of the other two detectives would take his information. Was this a delaying tactic? Easy to cover up involvement, incompetence, or corruption by appearing to help the police.

Now she only had June Sato. Frequent interference on a case was often an attempt to misdirect. Ordinary people did this hoping to distract the investigation until it was dropped. Real criminals knew it didn't work.

There was no doubt that the Sato Second was keeping secrets. Were those secrets about the case? Or were they about some other amoral shit?

Sofie didn't like being pushed or feeling anxious about talking to a suspect. Although she needed a lot more undeniable proof than she had if she was to suggest that June Sato was involved.

She hit the contact information on the message and sat. The stim Bindes gave her was wearing off and her legs were shaky.

Instead of reaching an aide, the call was answered by the Second personally. "Detective. I don't usually wait this long for someone to respond."

"The investigation takes priority," Sofie said. "I'm sure you prefer we find the killer." It was never easy to walk the knife-edge between respect and annoyance when you didn't actually feel someone in power deserved any deference. Sofie waited for a response, knowing she'd cross the line if she kept going.

"I expected more progress," June Sato said. "I haven't heard anything. Is that because you are stalled, or about to make an arrest?"

She would get the same answer as anyone who tried to get details. Having any names in the public was always a problem, whether they came from the media or from a well-meaning citizen.

"We have some leads to follow, and theories. We do need to tread carefully when we interrogate people. I'm sure you don't want any rumors to become associated with the Pratham's death." *Like his visits to the dark streets, for a start.*

"If you give me the names, perhaps I can expedite the flow of information." June Sato looked to the side and told someone to wait. "I am busy, but I can assign work to someone. If you need help, that is."

She wanted to control the investigation, but also didn't want the people of the Mallet to have any reason to suspect a cover-up. Not that it would change anything. Truth had little to do with whether the lower castes would blame the Elites. Or, maybe, June was feeling the restless mood of the station.

Sofie still didn't have anything she could share. And it would help later if June Sato seemed to know more than she'd been told.

"Please rest easy that we are on top of the investigation. It is vital that the case be clean in the eyes of the public. If we need help, there are other police employees who can be made available."

She didn't like to hear that. For all her reputation for being inscrutable and in control, June Sato displayed her emotions on her face as much as any person. Her eyes narrowed. She almost turned to the other person in the room. She took too long to think about her response. Too bad they would never get her in an interrogation room.

"There are things your commanders cannot provide. If you require any access that isn't within your reach, please ask. The Sato family needs this crime solved. The contest for the position of Pratham is distracting and unavoidable. It is important that we choose the right person."

And not someone who killed to get the position. Somehow Sofie couldn't believe it would matter.

"Is there someone we should be investigating?" It was worth a try. Even if June Sato wanted to throw someone under the bus, a name might shed light.

"You are not the only person who is constrained by rules, Detective. I cannot point you in any direction with confidence. I do not believe the killer is part of my family or any of the Elites."

Oh yes, she did. Too bad they would be off limits. If an Elite committed this crime, they'd find a useful tool to take the blame. Pay off any family members with money or promotion. Manufacture the evidence and express sorrow that someone would feel such anger at the kind and gentle families that shepherded the Mallet.

"Then we will continue with our case. I assure you we will do everything we can to find the killer. They will face the legal consequences."

June ended the call with a reminder not to wait as long before the next update.

24

"That went well," Rick said. "So, you think she knows who killed him?"

"If not that, I believe she knows why he was killed. And it must be bad if she's not willing to tell us." Sofie wondered why the Sato family hadn't already presented them with a culprit. Or had she hinted at a Pratham being the scapegoat earlier?

Amanda closed her pad. "Or it's still going on. You can't be sure he didn't have a partner in the family, or another one." She stretched. "I need to get out of here for a while. I'll follow up on some of our missing reports from central data."

It was getting late and tired cops made mistakes. "Let's pack it in," Sofie said to Rick. "Tomorrow we'll go back to tracking down Mitch."

Rick turned off the projector. "We should go look for the kill site. You know where it probably is since no one reported a bloody mess. We'll need more people."

"Tomorrow," Sofie said. She couldn't go back there today. "I'll send an update and request resources."

"You have to wonder what a Pratham was doing in the dark streets," Rick said.

It wasn't the right time to tell him what she'd learned. Her fingers were tingling. The damn meds were wearing off. There was definitely something wrong. If Bindes didn't figure out what it was, she'd make it her priority right after this case closed. She wasn't sure if that meant figuring out the meds problem, or having the operation, or both.

"Yeah, not that he wouldn't be involved in some of the business down there, but he'd have a lackey to do the in-person tasks." Sofie tucked her pad into her pocket. "Are you hanging around?"

Rick nodded to something behind her. "Visitor."

She turned. Haadiya Rothwell. Why did such a slime-ass look so good? Cheekbones that could slice bread, square jaw, piercing blue eyes — rare on the Mallet. If only his moral compass didn't spin like a wheel. As a member of the Executive, he made life easy for the Elites. Just like Nhu, he had his own agenda. Unlike Nhu, he would align with anyone to get a bit more status. The current state of the Sato family was probably his wet dream come true.

Haadiya tried to push open the door to the case room. It was sealed against anyone but the three of them. He frowned at her and stood back.

"If you want to go home, you need to get around him." Rick sat and pulled out his pad. "I'll wait until you send him away."

Being the case leader had its disadvantages.

Sofie checked to make sure there was nothing in the open to give away their progress or the direction of the case. All clear. She opened the door and stood aside for Haadiya to enter.

"I'll speak to your captain to get admission," he said. "An oversight on his part. I will forgive it this time."

Sofie would send a heads up to Llewelyn that the request was coming through. If he granted Haadiya Roth-well access, she'd be informed. Unlikely, but with notice they could sanitize this room and find another location to keep the real documents and theories. "How can we help you today, Haadiya?"

Maybe he was in the room to give some inside informa-tion, maybe to help sabotage a candidate for Pratham. If she had to guess, Sofie would put her money on both. It was up to them to sort out the useful information from the machi-nations of his ambition.

"Your investigation is taking a surprisingly long time." He waited for either her or Rick to fill in the pause. When neither spoke, he said, "You are aware that the longer it takes to put someone away for this crime the more chaos builds. Chaos in the Elite families always infects the station."

"Two days is not a long time," Rick said. "We have some direction now, but you understand we need to keep the information within the team. Can't let rumor add to the chaos."

Rick was good at handling Haadiya. Being a few inches taller than everyone on the Mallet gave him a measure of intimidation. And an excuse when someone accused him of arrogance.

"When do you think you'll be able to solve this unfortu-nate situation?" Haadiya asked. He pulled out one of the chairs and sat. "We all know it was someone in Mainte-nance, the people are too easily pushed to violence. Why haven't you brought anyone in for questioning at least?"

This couldn't turn into a long interrogation. Sofie felt the tingle in her fingers getting painful. She had maybe a half hour to swallow the meds before it turned into a full-blown attack, if she could keep her stress under control. "We expect to do that shortly," she said. "I'm sure you will receive an update as soon as there is information."

He looked at her and Sofie stilled. If he saw anything to reveal the Fades, he would have leverage to use against her. Being in his debt would be worse than losing her career.

"You have been in the battles," he finally said. "Concerning this case?"

"Sometimes following clues is a dangerous job," she said. "Even if it turns out to have nothing to do with the murder."

He stood, smoothed his hair, and scanned the room. He sniffed at the blank walls and empty tabletop. "Rumor has it that you think the body was moved."

Sofie didn't trust herself to answer. Keeping the investigation close didn't stop the sale of information.

Rick stood. "You know how rumors work, Haadiya. You've started enough of them. What if it's true? You have anything interesting to add?"

Haadiya walked to the door and pushed it open a few millimeters. "If it was, then you are looking for another location. I worry that you will pry into the wrong activities and that would be... dangerous for you." He looked at Sofie again, his gaze lingering on her injuries.

"We go where the leads take us," Sofie said. "If you have any information that will help the investigation, I hope you'll be frank with us. But we do have work to finish today."

He looked her over again. This behavior was far different from his usual inappropriate flirting. Someone or something was pushing him to change his methods.

"Very well, I hope your actions produce results before

someone else is killed. Oswald didn't like to work alone. He always had a partner who could take any blame. His partners often had fewer qualms about how they made their credits."

He left without looking back.

"What happened to you?" Rick asked. "I mean, since he brought it up."

"An argument with someone who didn't like me asking questions. No big deal." She tried to change the subject. "Why do you think the Elite families aren't just closing the case for us? They're applying enough pressure."

"Must think they have time to make the result look clean." He followed her out of the door. "What time do you want to start tomorrow?"

She couldn't face the dark streets again so soon. "Usual start. At the dump site? We can start there and work our way out."

25

"I couldn't find Mitch yesterday," Sofie said. She stood beside Rick at the familiar mech recess with the holo of the body lying on the floor. Last night she'd managed to get home and take the meds before it was too late. The tests came through just after she got home. Her condition was getting worse, but probably because the meds were too weak to keep it in check. Something that would reverse with the right dosage. A good sleep and she felt as healthy as someone who'd been beaten up could feel. "Maybe we start there."

Rick bent over the body and then flipped the holo. "If you're right and they used a dolly to move him, we should see some evidence." He knelt and looked closely at the rumples in Oswald's clothing.

"We still don't have the inventory," Sofie said. She pulled out her pad and sent a reminder to the manager, then joined Rick on the floor.

"Here," he said, pointing to a long fold in the jacket. "It's easy to dismiss all this mess on his clothes as coming from the floor. This could be from a strap."

How did I miss this? The Fades, of course. Too many distractions. And not all the symptoms are physical. "Look at this. If the first one is from a strap, then these are too. Broken up, but still in a line."

Using the first crease as a guide, they found a pattern that could be from the body being held on an upright transport. No need for restraints if he'd been laid flat on top of a mech.

"Okay, step back," Rick said. "Let me see if we can reconstruct."

This was Rick's strength, creating possible scenes. They'd caught more than a few criminals with his skill.

Sofie watched as Rick flipped Oswald's body to rock on its heels, like it was resting on a tipped-back dolly during transit. Then he added a holo of a few types of dollies until he found the one that fit. Sofie made a note of the model. It would come in handy when they got the inventory.

Rick moved the body holo onto the dolly one and they fit perfectly. He called up strapping that would be used and laid it across the crease patterns.

"Not quite," Sofie said. "Any other kinds?"

Rick didn't answer as he walked around the setup. Then he adjusted the body holo. "He wouldn't have been stiff when they moved him. If I slump the holo, it's perfect."

And it was. "Record it," Sofie said. "Send it back to the crime techs."

"What are you still doing here?" Mitch's voice startled Sofie. He stood on the sidewalk out of range of their work.

She stepped out of the recess to face him, hoping to see some evidence to explain his absence. A pallor from an illness, a few bruises maybe, but nothing showed. He was avoiding her, no doubt in her mind. "This is a crime scene," she said. "We don't go away until the murder is solved."

"But people live here," he said. "They deserve some peace."

Their investigation was quiet because they didn't want to attract any prying eyes or any media. "Who's been disturbing the peace? No one has tried to pass the barrier. If there are problems here, you need to tell us."

Mitch backed away a few steps and held his hands up in a placating gesture. "No one. I guess I mean people don't like having the cops around."

Rick turned off the holo and joined her. "Any reason someone is nervous when we're here?"

"Fuck, no. I misspoke. Give me a break." Mitch took a few more steps backward and then stood his ground.

"Where were you yesterday?" Sofie asked. "I came looking to follow up on that information. You were supposed to be on duty."

"I don't tell people my plans. This isn't the only area I look after. I sent that stuff to you. I can't help it if you lost it."

He was panicking. Sofie could tell from his face that all the bravado in his words was empty. Something was scaring him, and it wasn't her or Rick. Or, maybe they were the problem. Someone was threatening him because of them. Pushing harder would probably crank the fear up higher than it needed to be, and she didn't want to shut him down. "Okay, send it again. Now."

"I have to go back to my office." He took a step away.

"Use your pad," Rick said. "Or are you lying? If you sent it once, you can just find the link and send it again."

Mitch pulled out his pad and opened it. His hands shook as he slid his finger up the screen. Sofie couldn't see the details, but there were a lot of unread messages.

"When did you send it?" Rick asked as he moved around behind Mitch to peer over his shoulder.

Mitch turned the screen away. "Hey, there's confidential information here." He kept flicking through the list.

Too many messages for a legitimate supervisor job. Mitch had something on the side that he didn't want brought out into the open. It could come in handy for leverage later.

"Here." He tapped one of the highlighted lines. "Shit, it looks like it got stalled." One quick tap and Sofie heard her own pad ping. "Anything else? I have a busy day ahead of me."

She opened the message and saw a list of names and bullet points with random notes and comments. This would take some work to collate. She sent it to Amanda and then nodded to Rick. He moved to stand beside her.

"One more thing," she said. "Two actually. Don't disappear on me again. If I'm looking for you, I need to find you. Okay?"

"You have my contact number. I'll answer."

She didn't believe him, but it wasn't worth the effort to argue the point. "We weren't able to find a few people on the list yesterday. You know anything about that?"

"Who?"

"Zim and Lyman." *Do so many people go missing in his section that he can't remember names?*

"I was looking for them yesterday, too. Both gone. The Zim woman and the parents in that Lyman family. Lazy assholes. Probably holed up somewhere drinking their wages away."

It wasn't his job to be sympathetic, but even Mitch must know there was a difference between malingering and mourning a missing child. "Had problems with them before?"

Mitch closed his mouth on whatever he was about to tell

her. After a moment's thought, he said, "Not much with the Zim woman. She's pretty stubborn and doesn't just do as she's told. I guess nothing serious on the others either, just the usual complaining about life. You find them, let me know?"

"Did you report them missing?" Rick asked. "So someone official starts looking?"

"I was getting to that," Mitch said. "If we're done here, I got work to take care of."

26

"He's definitely up to something shady," Rick said when Mitch was out of sight. "Maybe nothing to do with the case, but I've got that creepy feeling we're missing something."

"Did you get a look at any of the headlines on his pad? Lot of messages for his kind of job." Sofie reached into the recess and turned off the holo.

"He's running some kind of book. Betting on quotas, injuries, small stuff like that. Not enough to explain what I'm feeling."

"We'll figure it out if it's important." She glanced around but nothing jumped out at her to solve the case. Sometimes it happened. A tiny detail became clear at the most unexpected time. They wouldn't get that kind of luck today.

"Any interest in getting a ton of backup and searching the dark streets?" Rick asked.

Not yet, Sofie thought. "Can you arrange that? For later today. Mitch gave me an idea."

He glanced at her neck and Sofie pulled up her collar to cover the bruise.

"Is it going to result in any more of that?"

"You think I need protecting?" The words were out before she thought. It was hard to argue she didn't need help when her neck was black-and-blue.

"No. You need your partner. You go off by yourself all day and we don't know where you are. Clearly something happened."

"It was nothing." She wanted this conversation to end. Rick was a good partner but sometimes he wanted to know more about her private life than she wanted to share. "I need to follow this lead alone. My source won't show if I bring you along."

"I'm your partner. It's my job to protect you, like it's yours to have my back," he said. "Next time just let me know what you're up to. I won't stop you."

She laughed. "Okay, I promise I won't do it again. If I need to go out alone because you'll get in my way, I'll leave all kinds of clues for you to follow."

He didn't move away to let her past.

"What?" She didn't have time for whatever he was up to.

"This *is* the next time, Sofie. Where are you going?"

"Okay, you might have a point about me. I'm going to the Temporaries. There's only one way for someone to escape the Mallet. If those parents or the killers are trying to leave, they have to be smuggled."

He stood aside. "Okay, the worst that can happen is you get drunk and have a good time."

Their paths split a few minutes later. Rick's parting words were an order to return to the office by one. If she'd thought he was serious with this big brother act, she'd have taken him down to training and kicked his ass.

The Temporaries on this end of the station were not far,

but she'd have to keep track of time to make it back to the office by one. She'd met Torque, her contact in the Temporaries, at a party a few years ago. He worked for one of the giant mining corporations that used the Mallet for refining and distributing their product.

The designation for Temporaries had nothing to do with the length of time they stayed on the Mallet. The fact that they could leave without permission was the key. This half of the section was where people could be smuggled out for a price. The other half, what the locals called the mouth of the Mallet, was where people, drugs, contraband, and ideas flowed in. Sofie didn't know which was more dangerous, ideas or drugs and contraband.

There was always a party in this section. People with no ties, high wages and little to occupy themselves needed a release. Sofie preferred they drink, dance, and copulate their spare time away, rather than agitate and fight. Whoever unofficially ran the section kept things in control. Much like the dark streets, but a lot less deadly. She suspected Torque was one of the people who kept the peace.

Something new made her pause. Usually, you just wandered in and out of the section. Today, three people barred the entrance, checking IDs and turning a few people away.

She walked up to face the first of the gatekeepers. "What's going on?" If they were keeping secrets, maybe she should be looking closer at the people inside.

"Hey, Sofie," the young girl said. "You go right ahead."

"Evie, what's with the guards? You have trouble?"

The girl looked around her but didn't call for assistance. "We've had a few people bringing attitude in lately, and we've broken up a couple of fights. So they got banned. And we don't want their friends in, either. Mallet people are angry about something. So we check ID, and it keeps the mood happy on the streets."

The workers in the Temporaries didn't see themselves as Mallet people. She always figured they had it right; Temporaries could leave, but Mallet residents were here for life.

"You could report them," Sofie said, feeling obliged to offer the help. She scanned the area around her. It wasn't crowded with people too drunk or drugged to know better than to start a fight. Sure, there were a few more people hanging about than she expected at this time of shift, but maybe they were here for the entertainment value of Evie and her friends acting as guards while wearing very little clothing.

Evie bubbled out a giggle. "We got it, no need for the heavies. You in for a party?" She turned her attention to the people on the street behind Sofie.

If she said she was on official business, would Evie turn her away? It wouldn't keep her out, but the paperwork would be a pain, and the relationship between the cops and the Temporaries would be damaged. "Just want a chat with Torque. Hoping he knows something to help me out."

"Torque's no snitch," Evie said without taking her eyes off the street behind Sofie.

"I'm not asking him for that," Sofie said. "And he can tell me to fuck off all by himself if he needs to."

Evie laughed again. "So he can. Go ahead. It's switch day, so you might have a bit of a challenge tracking him down."

Switch day was the scheduled transport day. Anyone wanting out left on a transport specifically provided for the purpose by the different employers off-station. Farewell parties vied with welcome bashes to make the most noise and fun.

"Thanks for reminding me," Sofie said. "I'll see you when I leave."

Evie nodded and stepped aside to challenge a man behind Sofie.

27

The party going on at the entrance had a frantic feel to it that Sofie didn't remember from previous visits. She only had so much time before Rick would be nagging her to return. Torque could be anywhere — well, at any party. She twisted her way between groups of people who were too desperately trying to have fun to notice her. Maybe they wanted to leave but were denied passage.

The Mallet didn't care when they moved along or arrived. Their employers were a different matter. People signed contracts. Sofie had seen one a few years ago. It amounted to indentured servitude. Yes, they may have a lot of freedom compared to the inhabitants of the station, but even a party could be a prison. She'd asked Torque about it when he was flying high. Not all contracts were that way, apparently; some people had special skills or special contacts, and fewer obligations.

The layout here was the same as every part of the station. Streets joined in small squares lined with retail stores and pubs and the occasional private school. At the first square, Sofie stepped up onto a stool to see over the heads of the crowd, a bouncing sea of multicolored hair and jewels. The individuals seeming to meld together into one happy, altered state.

Across the square she spotted Torque. Short, stout, and in his usual business attire, he was passing out pills to anyone who walked by. His blue hair was tied up in a topknot, his nose ring had charms glinting from it, and his gold tooth caught the light when he laughed. None of that made him stand out as much as his skin. White, like he'd been born in the dark and never come out.

She couldn't catch his attention from her perch so she dropped back to the street and wiggled through the crowd in as straight a line as she could make happen. Someone offered her a drink, smoke, or pill every few steps. Each was greeted with a smile and a shake of her head. No point in trying to be heard over the music.

In what felt like the middle of the square, too many people blocked her way, so she turned right toward the perimeter sidewalk, hoping it would be clearer. The music felt like it was pounding on her skin and inside her body. She slipped past a group of people dressed as some kind of mythical creatures, all wings, haloes, and feathers. Sofie breathed in before she noticed the orange mist of psychoactive drugs. She spat out the taste and moved faster.

The bodies around her took on a softer shape, as though they really were melting together. She pushed her hands ahead of her to create a wedge path. It rippled the air and people melted away. Her fingers tingled and she giggled.

She could see the sidewalk, it was only steps away, and then it was beyond far. The station wasn't big enough to hold it. Then she wandered through a fine rain of purple dust. Reality snapped back and everything had the right dimensions, all sharp and clear.

She stepped onto the sidewalk. Her fingers still tingled. *Fuck.*

An attack of the Fades here wouldn't bring anyone's attention because they were all involved in their own party. But falling could get her trampled, and a full-on blackout? Too many people here to predict what might happen. She pressed against the nearest building as her hands started to tremble. The alley. It would have a recess.

Sofie stumbled to the dark corner. Leaning in, she saw the recess was empty. And people had tossed in wrappers from their mind-twisting entertainment of choice. Someone had tossed in a cloak with sequins and colorful patches. She crawled in and pulled the cloak over her, hoping the weight would be enough to stop her leaving the recess while she was blacked out. Reaching into her pocket, she pulled out three of the meds Bindes had given her and tossed them into her mouth. If one didn't last, maybe three would stop or shorten the attack and keep her safe for long enough.

The music still pounded but now her body didn't feel like it was part of a percussion instrument. She could feel her symptoms wash away. She could also feel weariness pull her to sleep. She set her pad to wake her in fifteen minutes, hoping the attack was mild enough to let the vibrations register on her unconscious mind. She closed her eyes and let reality slip into dreams.

THE VIBRATIONS from her pad broke through the nightmare of being lost in a storm of sound. Sofie opened her eyes. She knew who she was and why she was here — a good sign. She assessed her body. No lingering symptoms.

She stood and brushed off the bits of detritus that stuck to her from the floor and the cloak. She needed to blend in when she left to find Torque, and looking like she'd slept in a dirty recess wasn't the image she wanted to project. And even though she felt safe, Sofie wanted to be sure, so staying in the recess for a few minutes seemed like a good idea.

She itched to open the chute and drop everything in, but the mech would be by soon enough. The cloak was good enough quality that someone might come looking for it, so she hung it on a protrusion to stop the mech sweeping it into the recycle system.

Inhalers, wrappers, and other drug debris made up most of the mess. A couple of empty plastic drink bottles and the broken wing from someone's costume sat in a corner. Sofie lifted the wing and placed it in the center of the recess to facilitate the clear out. A gleam caught her eye. Not garbage, not something tossed to the side after fulfilling its purpose. A ring. She put on gloves and picked it up carefully. Oswald Sato's ring, to be precise.

28

She examined Sato's ring. No blood, nothing to indicate it had been removed violently. Why would he leave it here? Did he give it to someone who tossed it after the news of his death got out? Or had someone placed it here while she was unconscious?

Why wasn't the Sato family asking for it to be found? And how was she going to convince anyone, even herself, that this wasn't all planned? That someone hadn't managed everything from the moment she entered the party to when she crawled into the recess?

Maybe Torque could answer these questions. She sent a request to the scene techs to discreetly examine the recess. She needed more than this to authorize a full-scale search of the Temporaries. The area held a version of an embassy status.

She debated waiting for the techs, but decided finding Torque was more critical to solving the case. The drug she'd inhaled in the party had affected more than her vision. The trip it sent her on wasn't the few moments she'd thought.

She'd been stumbling through the partiers for almost an hour before the attack.

She set a barrier at the entrance to the recess and entered a report of what actions she'd taken so they could eliminate her trace, leaving out any mention of her nap under the cloak. She stepped out to the street.

The party had moved along by the time she headed back to the square. She slipped an inhaler on her face to prevent any further accidental highs. Torque was nowhere to be seen, but she knew a handful of places he liked to hang out. She checked her messages as she crossed the square to the first one. Rick, four messages. She wasn't quite late for the meeting, but maybe he had news. She hit return call.

"Where are you?" He didn't waste time with any small talk, so he was worried.

"Temporaries. Looking for my contact. Why are you calling?" She peeked in the door of the first pub Torque liked to frequent. Not there. "Can you do the dark streets search by yourself? I found something here I need to follow up on."

"Couldn't get permission to go in without more concrete links. We could go together and find it without making it official."

She was embarrassed by the relief that flooded her at not having to go back — yet. "I'll send the details on my discovery. Maybe you can meet the tech team there. Someone needs to stop them expanding out to the whole section."

"I got the notification. Sure. I'll be there. You can come find me when you're done."

He thought he was missing out on something interesting. If he came with her, Torque wouldn't tell her anything. He seemed to think they had a special relationship. They didn't, but she was happy to let him think so. "I'll tell you everything I learn. You know informants, they're twitchy. Anything new?"

She turned down a side street toward the outports. Torque's official job was manager of the outgoing transits. He tended to 'manage from a distance' as he called it. But there were restaurants he frequented that might prove fruitful during this part of the shift.

"Nothing," Rick said. "Your equipment friend has disappeared, so we put in a new order for the data."

"You putting any money on us getting anything other than some unexpected glitch wiping the data for the time in question?" She looked through the window of the first restaurant. No Torque.

"Only bet I'm taking is on how long it will take. You think this guy wiped it and is in hiding?"

"I think he knew who took the dolly and why, or he was the one who moved the body. He already tried to blame it on the blip. Add him to the list of people we need to find."

"Okay. Send me anything you have on that scene for the techs. I'll keep the team quiet unless we find some reason to go public."

Sofie didn't have much hope they could keep it confidential. The Satos would have a mole somewhere in the crime scene group, which was probably where Haadiya got his information. "I'll let you know when I'm done. Ask them for a holo ASAP."

"Yep."

She saw Torque's blue hair over the top of a booth in the next restaurant. He saw her coming and jerked his head at the person across from him, who slid out and went to sit at the bar.

"Torque," she said as she joined him. "Looking good."

"I can't say the same about you. Get beaten up again?"

Sofie turned down the waiter's offer of a drink and pulled up the list of missing people on her pad. "Hazard of the job in some places. You know anything about these people?"

"I hope you aren't suggesting the Temporaries are anything but a peaceful and loving place." He leaned in to read the list.

"Always a party here," she said. "The names?"

"None of them come to mind. What's the story?"

He didn't usually play games. If he didn't know, or didn't want to tell her, he was usually up-front about it. "You know about the Sato murder?"

"What does that have to do with us?"

"I'm trying to figure it out. All the people on the list have mysteriously disappeared. They might be involved. Any chance a few of your cargo manifests missed reporting some mystery organics?"

"Not recently, and no criminals ever."

He conveniently ignored the fact that smuggling people was a crime, and for most of the residents of the Mallet, leaving without permission was a crime.

"What about Sato? You know anything that might explain the murder?"

He took a long sip of his drink and glanced over her shoulder to scan the restaurant. Then he met her eyes, and Sofie could see him considering the risk of lying to her.

"You've known me a long time, Torque. As long as you aren't involved, you're safe. No one official knows you talk to me. Nothing has changed yet. If we don't solve the murder, I can't promise that will continue."

"I hear things are rougher than usual outside our doors. You'll be more likely to find answers out there." He drained the glass and then pushed it away. "He came here to make commercial arrangements. You don't want to mess with that."

"He had a partner?" The only reason the arrangements would still be active. "Was he murdered because the partner got greedier?"

"I don't know any details. He didn't deal with me. I have... compunctions about some things. Before you ask, I don't know who the partner is, but if I had to guess, he's dead because of his business, not his partner. The Pratham was the brains."

"Who can tell me about the business? Or the partner?"

"All I have is rumor. And it's the kind that is more a warning to stay away than it is details on the racket."

She had the feeling he wanted to tell her something but needed her to ask the right question. Sofie had no idea what that was. And forcing him would dry up the flow of other information. He was too valuable to waste on something she'd eventually solve herself. There was one thing she could dig into. "Most of the people on that list are parents of missing children. Does that make a difference?"

"To what? I told you I don't know anything. Missing kids are a tragedy, but I can't tell you what I don't know."

So that wasn't the magic question. "I hope I don't learn anything that proves you lied to me."

29

S ofie reached out to Rick. If she was going to get back to Maintenance without being dragged into the tech work, she needed him to cooperate, because sneaking past him created two problems. One was that he wouldn't let it go and she'd hear about skipping the boring parts of the investigation forever. The other, more important one was that she probably didn't have that kind of luck and he'd look up and catch her tiptoeing past.

"I'm going to hunt Mitch down and take him in for questioning," she said. "My source didn't have anything concrete."

"Waste of time? Or more vague hints?"

"Oswald was up to something shady, and he had a partner who might have killed him to keep the profits, and is still running the op."

She waited for Rick to say he'd join her.

"We're done here. There was nothing useful. I'll drop the ring into the evidence vault. You want some help interrogating Mitch?"

"Stick around headquarters in case I do, but I think he

finds me scarier than you." The ring was a problem. The Sato family could force a search of the Temporaries, but they did a lot of business out here, not all of it on the dark side of moral. If the investigation caused interruptions in the flow of money, or endangered their contracts with off-station corporations, they might just write off the Pratham's death, name their scapegoat, and move on. "I hope the case doesn't point us back here."

"No. I don't think anyone has the skills to walk that tightrope. Let me know when you need me."

She slipped her pad into a pocket and strode out to Maintenance. The fastest way to get Mitch into an interrogation room was to request a track on his ID. Fast was relative; the paperwork needed to get the track started was monumental.

She skirted the dark streets on her way to Mitch's official section. The gatekeepers were still on duty, different faces from the ones who dragged her out. If the kill site was in there, life would be much easier. People were used to all kinds of violence in the dark streets.

Mitch wasn't hiding. Sofie escorted him from a conversation at a stim bar, sent a report that he was assisting her so a replacement would be assigned, and had him seated in a room at headquarters within twenty minutes.

"Why all the formality, Detective?" Mitch said. "I have been doing my best to help you. It's not my fault I don't know anything."

"Yeah, we're past that now. You know something about this crime. If you don't start telling me everything, I'll arrest you as an accessory and inform the Sato Second that you delayed justice for their Pratham. Can I get you stim?" She liked to keep people off-kilter. Threat followed by kindness was the best way she'd found to do that. And Mitch needed a few minutes to consider what would happen if she followed through on the threat.

"No. We won't be here long," Mitch said. "I don't know where you got the idea I'm holding back, because I've told you everything I know. I took the time to gather the information I sent you on the missing people."

Information that hasn't helped us find them or the killer. "The Satos won't believe you. They're looking for a scapegoat."

He swallowed. "Where is my advocate?"

"You don't need one. You aren't under arrest — yet."

"Then I'm free to go." He didn't move.

"Yep. Of course, I'll be forced to report your incompetence to your boss."

He stiffened but didn't speak.

Sofie waited him out. If she made that report, he'd be back on the line with the people he'd been bullying, cheating, and extorting — an accident waiting to happen.

"What proof will you make up?" He fidgeted with his sleeves, pulling them over his hands and then back. "I'm not incompetent."

"Something like a murder happened in your section and you know nothing about it? Surely that's not how they expect you to keep order."

"And if I do know something about the murder?" He looked up and shook his head at what he saw on her face. "Not who did it. Maybe nothing that will help you find the killer, but something."

"It all goes away."

He stared at his hands for a long time. Sofie sat back and folded her arms across her chest. If he was trying to come up with a lie or present his information in a way that hid his involvement, she needed to hear it before she tore it apart.

He sighed and then looked at her. "The body was placed in the recess."

"Why?" He wouldn't have done that himself. If Mitch moved the body, it would have been to another supervisor's section. Unless there was a very compelling reason to implicate himself.

"I owe some debts to the boss of the dark streets. He said I was even if I let them dump the body. I had no choice." His voice was quiet — not with shame, but fear. Scared that his deal was void?

"Where in the dark streets?" She really didn't want to go back, but if it put an end to this case, she'd do it. "Try telling me you don't know. See how that works. You picked it up, right?"

"I can draw you a map. I can't go back there."

"Tell me what you saw."

"Blood. Probably still there, no one seemed to be cleaning up. They took a few things. I guess to throw you off."

That explains the ring and why it was so easy to find. "Who was there?"

"Three of them. All covered up. I can't identify them. Maybe two men and a boy or a woman."

She liked this part of the process. The point where the suspect just couldn't stop talking. "What did they say?"

"Told me to take the body. Told me to keep you busy. Said someone was going to pay well for the experience."

Her stomach sank at the thought that 'the experience' meant sex on a Pratham's blood. It wouldn't be worth the punishment to kill a Pratham for that purpose, but taking advantage of an existing situation was what she expected from the dark streets boss.

The crime techs were going to be busy. And down there, they'd need protection.

"That's all I know." Mitch made to rise.

"Stay here. Draw the map. We'll see what happens when I get a look at this location."

"They will know I talked."

"Probably."

He settled back in the chair. "I guess I'm safer here than out there. I'll take that stim now. I like blufroot in mine."

Sofie gave his order to the officer standing outside the door. Mitch deserved a little treat for his effort. Time to put pressure on the captain to organize the search team.

30

Sofie led Rick and six large, heavily-armed officers into the dark streets. Whether the boss of this section knew they were coming or not didn't matter. She had her location and protection.

Rick answered his pad, acknowledged whatever the person said, and put it away. "The crime scene guys are with their guards and waiting for our go-ahead."

"Let's hope we won't have to send them away." She checked her own pad. The DNA test app was ready. Knowing it was Oswald Sato's blood would be enough to bring on the full forensic investigation. In any other section of the Mallet, it would be easier. In here? No one wanted to be the one to ignite whatever violent reaction the boss felt necessary.

"Someone should have spaced these guys before they got too powerful," the officer behind her said.

"They exist because they have customers," Sofie said. "Space these ones, and the next will be less open about their location. But that's really the only leverage we have, I guess."

She let the armed guard take position around the

mouth of the recess before walking in. It was identical to the place they found the body. All mech recesses were standard design. This one looked like a kill site. The blood wasn't a surprise. She'd smelled it a block away. The fact that it was still here was the shock. She didn't think they'd made even a token effort to hide the evidence. "This wasn't done by a local," she said. "This was left here as leverage over someone, probably everyone who even looked at the gore. 'Do what I say, or I'll send the images to the Sato family'. No one wants to be noticed by an Elite."

"Is the blood his?" Rick asked.

Sofie opened the bag containing the equipment she'd been taught to use. A sliver of plastic to scoop a sample of the dry blood, a dropper with some kind of liquid to reconstitute it so it could be smeared over the bullseye on her pad screen, and a wet cloth to clear her pad after. She had no idea how it worked to identify the DNA, but she'd been assured it was accurate.

She followed the procedure and her phone flashed *Pratham Oswald Sato, Deceased.*

"Here we go," she said. One tap sent the results to Captain Llewelyn and the crime scene team.

"A delegation is approaching," the officer who'd spoken earlier said. "Do you want me to keep them away?"

"Let's not go out of our way to cause friction," Sofie said. "We'll be out in a second."

Rick pointed to items strewn around the recess. "His things. Still here, in the dark streets where anything that can be sold is. It's a message for someone: don't mess with us."

Sofie waved him to follow her out to meet whoever waited for them. Three dark streets residents. One of the people who dealt with her attacker and two strangers. None of them bore anything that looked like a weapon. That didn't mean they weren't dangerous.

"The boss sent us," the first man said.

They don't want to be here. I guess no one refuses an order without consequences. "You have something to tell me?"

"No one who lives here did this. We'll let you investigate without interference. The boss wants this wrapped up fast. Your presence is bad for business. We don't want what's going on in Maintenance to stir up trouble here."

He didn't wait for an answer. The three marched away and turned the corner.

"Interesting," Rick said.

"We need to look at this before the team gets here. If there are clues left after all this time, I don't want them tied up in the lab."

"I'll record. You search?" Rick pulled out his pad.

As much as she wanted to avoid going back inside the recess, Sofie was the worst holo-recorder on the force. She had Rick make a baseline while she applied as much protection as she could manage. Gloves, shoe covers, and a fixer spray so she wouldn't contaminate the scene.

"Let me know when you want to take something away." Rick set up just to the side of the entrance.

The crime techs preferred the scene be kept pristine. The cops always wanted to take evidence as soon as possible. The procedures required her to leave a holo of any removed items.

Sofie took one more look in the space before stepping in and starting her narration. Nothing jumped out as important, except that no one had stolen everything. The ring had been taken to misdirect them to the Temporaries and the Sato family would need an inventory to tell if anything was missing, but everything should have disappeared into the black market within minutes of the body leaving the space. If anything was still here, the boss wanted them to find it.

"The blood is concentrated in more or less the center of the space," Sofie said. "Some evidence of spray has been smudged, possibly when the body was moved. No evidence of a mech attempting to work. Items scattered around, unlikely to have fallen from pockets. It is possible they are displayed for some purpose. No evidence of any activity in the recess since the murder. What appears to be normal, random detritus is scattered to the edges of the blood pools."

She listed the items she could see at a surface inspection. "Bracelet with ID chips embedded, empty flask, one black glove, possibly silk. No evidence of a credit chip."

It was weird not to ask Rick for his opinion, but this holo needed to be factual, so no conversations to muddy the data. She stepped to the far corner of the recess, trying unsuccessfully not to disturb any of the blood.

"One partial footprint from Detective Sofie Allen, will leave the shoe cover at the site as required."

She crouched down and lifted the edges of the garbage. Empty food packages, used wipes, random papers. She found a data film. It would be easy to slip it out without recording it, so no one would know they'd seen it. She'd log it later if there was any usable evidence on it. If she did, they would have time to search it for information without worrying about someone leaking it to the media or the Elite families. But that information might not be usable in the case against the murderer if it wasn't logged at the scene.

"One data film, approximately two centimeters square. Please create a holo, Detective Holdom. We will need to scan this."

She placed the film on her gloved fingertip and held it

still for Rick to record, then turned it over to capture the other side.

"Done," Rick said. "Anything else?"

"Nothing apparent." Sofie stepped out of the recess, pulled her glove off around the film and placed it in her pocket, then removed her shoe covers and placed them to the side of the entrance.

She addressed the officer who seemed to be in charge. "We'll leave now. Protect the scene and then assist the crime techs when they arrive."

"You safe to leave?" he asked.

"I think our messengers conveyed that," she said.

31

"We can't load the data film at work," Rick said. "Not until we know what's on there."

Too much risk of raising an alarm or having the film wiped for security, Sofie thought.

"Your place?" Sofie asked. She didn't want anyone in her quarters without notice.

"Yeah, it might not be empty yet."

"You leave your latest conquest alone in your quarters?" Rick avoided long term dates, but Sofie couldn't believe he trusted someone alone in his home. He must have secrets, everyone did.

"She was asleep, and I had to come out early. I'd rather not check and find her moved in. Can we do yours?"

Sofie tried to remember what was sitting on the small table when she left her quarters. She couldn't guarantee that there were no meds in plain view. "Okay," she said. If anything was on display that she didn't want him to see, she'd have to be fast. "I don't have any refreshments."

"You have the unconnected pad," Rick said as he started

moving toward her place. "We won't be long, right? A quick look and then back to headquarters."

Sofie didn't take the time to argue. In the fifteen minutes it would take to get to her quarters, she could think of a way to clean up before Rick entered. It didn't need to be a polite excuse after all, simply a believable one.

She opened the unit door and stepped inside. "Give me a sec," she said, blocking Rick from entering. He stood in the doorway, checking out the street.

Just as she feared, the pack of meds was on the table. She swept it into her hand and then dropped the bag into a drawer.

"Ready?" Rick asked.

"Come on in. Grab a chair from the corner and we'll look at the data film." Her small quarters were much like what they'd inspected in Maintenance. The difference was the furnishings were less shabby and the mattress a little thicker on the bed. Sofie didn't believe in spending her hard-earned credits on luxuries and didn't have visitors often. The small table sat against the far wall. The bathroom was a closed off closet at the other end of the same wall. Her bed occupied the facing wall along with a small table and a stim-juice machine.

"Where's your pad?" Rick asked, looking around.

She reached into the same drawer she'd just dropped the meds into and pulled out a personal pad that she'd paid to have disconnected from the network.

"You should get some nice stuff," Rick said, sitting and holding out the data film.

"Waste of money," Sofie said. She reached over to enter her code to unlock the device. "I'm hardly here to enjoy sleeping, let alone decorating."

He applied the data film to the screen and waited. "You spending your money on something else?"

"Maybe." He might have noticed her hiding the meds, but Sofie wasn't going to volunteer anything.

"Holy shit," Rick said. "This is everything."

Sofie leaned in to check the screen. A list of Oswald's off-the-books business activities. A couple of videos and a long list of text files.

"He was taking kids," Sofie said. "Not buying them from their parents, but just taking them." She pointed at a column filled with alphanumeric codes. "Looks like five different income streams from this alone." She tried not to think about what those could be.

"Drugs." Rick pointed at a file. "He was into the new stuff that might actually end up as illegal."

"Some legit ones too." Sofie noticed her own meds on the list of products the Satos controlled. "But that should be under the family, not his individual dealings."

They were going to need the resources back at the office. And Amanda. This was enough to point the way, but to resolve the case, to find the killer, they needed more detail about the crimes they'd found.

Rick played the video. Oswald talking to someone off-screen. He couldn't know he was being recorded.

You get your cut when the product reaches the buyer.

He sounded annoyed, like he'd said the same thing more than once. The response from the other person was fuzzed out. This was intended as leverage against the Pratham. The other person was a fool to think it would keep them safe.

If you want more, you find the kids and the buyers. You take a few risks.

Another buzzed out response. Then the video cut out.

Rick sat back, staring at the screen.

Sofie watched him digest the implications. When there were a few clues and a gut feeling, she didn't want to push him or influence his conclusions. She hoped desperately that her partner would come up with a different interpretation. Other than a Pratham selling off kids, and another mystery person still running the show. Someone very high in the organization who may be untouchable.

"We need to scan the film for anything that will trigger alarms at HQ," he finally said. "Malware, or even an ID code that alerts the Sato family or his partner. We need someone to dig into the information and find us details we can work on."

Sofie took the pad and ran the usual protection scans. Nothing came up. Whoever put the film there for them to find also meant for them to use it.

"Where do you think we should start looking?" she asked as the last few scans completed.

"The parents," Rick said. "If someone stole my kids and sold them, I'd kill."

"Hypothetically, right?"

"Yeah, since I don't have kids," Rick said. "And I guess not all parents are going to react the same way."

"It doesn't take all of them," Sofie said. "In the right circumstances one person could have murdered Oswald Sato. Drugged him first to make him compliant."

"I suppose," he said. He looked at her, then the drawer where her meds were hidden. "Speaking of hypothetically, if you have a drug problem I need to know."

So, he had seen her move the package.

"I don't have a drug problem." Not exactly true, but he hadn't meant if her medication was failing. He meant a recreational drug problem.

"Okay, but if something like that is going on, you need to

deal with it fast." He looked for a moment like he was going to say something more. Like, "or I'll report you." But he didn't.

If Sofie argued with him, she might end up saying something about the Fades, and that would be giving him a hold on her. But she needed him to stop worrying about her, so she had to say something. "Rick, I promise I don't have a problem with drugs. I took the same training as you. Drugs might be legal, but they still affect your response time and your ability to think under pressure. Not my bag. You know I don't even like to get drunk at a party."

"Every drug-addled officer took that training."

"Stop. You might not mind your private life being on display, but I do. I swear I don't have an addiction. You are safe with me."

"You forget I'm an excellent investigator. I know you're hiding something, but I'll believe you for now." He lifted the data film and tucked it in an evidence holder. "Okay. Let's get back to the office. I have a good feeling about this. We might solve this today."

The subject of her possible addiction was closed for today. Sofie noticed him glance at the drawer containing the meds. At least he was honest about not believing her. She'd be more careful in the future, and soon she'd have the operation, because she couldn't see any other way out, and then her denials would be true.

"It depends on what you mean by solve," she said. "I'm guessing the murder is the only crime that might ever get closed."

32

I t was late enough that the bullpen would be empty. Sofie sent a request to Amanda to wait for them. They needed fast action and no official attention for a couple of hours.

As soon as they stepped through the doorway, Llewelyn shouted, "Allen, Holdom, in my office, now."

Captain Llewelyn never stayed this late. A perk of being in charge. He didn't sound angry, and Sofie couldn't think of anything she'd done since their last meeting that would piss him off.

"Don't mention the data film unless he already knows," she whispered to Rick.

"Should I get it to Amanda?" Rick asked. "If she can get started, we might have a chance to find something concrete before it's shut down."

"He's watching, so no."

Rick knew as well as she did that the information they'd found would be suppressed. They couldn't keep it quiet long, but until they plugged into the network it was still a secret.

The captain was sitting behind his desk by the time they arrived. "Good work in finding the kill site," he said. "I'm sure it won't be long before forensics finds the killer."

Sofie took a seat and nodded to Rick to sit in the other chair. She wanted Llewelyn to see them as happy with the progress. He wasn't stupid, and if there was any hint of more information, he'd dig it out.

"I'm sure they'll find something," she said. "We still need to be cautious. The site was open to anyone who happened by for days."

"Don't be so pessimistic. You found the kill site. You'll find the killer. The case will close, and you can take a day or two to celebrate." Llewelyn turned his attention to Rick. "What do you think, Holdom? Will we be telling the Satos a result before their election is over?"

"You taught me not to get ahead of the evidence," Rick said. "It's a big step forward, I'll admit."

Llewelyn seemed happy about the find. He couldn't know about the data film. Sofie was sure he'd ask for it, or demand they enter it into evidence, or want to review the contents with them.

Someone created that video and left it for them to find. Oswald was unlikely to be carrying around evidence of his crimes. Even an Elite would be forced to answer for taking children. Not out of some feeling that kids were off limits, but because they were future resources. The names on the list of kids represented too many workers who wouldn't be contributing in the future.

"Do you need to report to the Satos?" Sofie asked. "They must be quite invested in the outcome."

"That's not for you to worry about," Llewelyn said. "I'm doing what I can to keep you free of external interference. It's not just the Elites, although all the families have reached out now. The media have been asking for a comment. The murder is too public to keep secret for long."

So, yes.

Sofie didn't respond. The less the Sato family knew about what they found, the better. The candidates for Pratham were on the suspect list. Along with the mysterious partner, the other Elite families, the parents of the kids, the buyers, and half the station. She told herself she was doing Llewelyn a favor by not telling him.

"We have some work to do," she said. "The preliminary results will be ready by now. Our observations need to be transcribed."

"I'll let you get to it, then." Llewelyn glanced at his screen. "Glad you dropped that missing kids thing and fully committed to the murder."

"Yes. I hate it when an investigation goes down a false trail, but that's pretty normal." She nodded to Rick to go ahead of her. "We'll report when we have something new."

Llewelyn seemed to have lost interest. He waved at them to get on with it and kept his attention on the screen.

Rick headed to the case room. Sofie could see Amanda watching them. "You think she'll agree to keep this quiet?" Sofie murmured.

"Do we have a choice?" Rick stopped by the stim-juice machine. "We need her skills. If she sees a benefit for herself, she'll agree. If she says she'll keep it under wraps, I don't think she'll lie."

Sofie hoped he was right. "I'll get the drinks, you go prep Amanda. She likes you better than me."

Rick laughed and walked away. Sofie set the machine for three large, hot stim-juices and loaded a handful of flavorings on a tray. The day had taken a lot out of her. She drew a cold stim-juice and glanced around before slipping a med into her palm. She couldn't risk an attack now. If the meds were weaker than usual, she should be fine taking more of them. If not, she'd have a few days to ride out the attack that waited for her when she stopped boosting the dose.

She observed Amanda and Rick as she approached the room. Nothing defensive in either of them. If Rick already told her about the contents of the data film and the need for secrecy, she'd agreed. If not, Sofie couldn't delay any longer.

She pushed the door open with her hip and put the drinks on the table. "Set windows to private, please."

Amanda touched an icon on her pad and the bullpen disappeared behind darkened windows. No one could look in, and they couldn't look out. Not ideal, but the door was also locked to prevent access to anyone who didn't have the right codes. Sofie hoped the captain had kept those to himself and the three people in the room.

"So we found something," Sofie said. "Did Rick tell you?"

Amanda glared at Rick. "No, he was busy flirting. Softening me up for something shady?"

Sofie wished they didn't need her. No matter if Amanda swore to keep their secret, the more people in the know, the more risk of it getting out. She put a flavor package into her stim-juice without looking, took a breath, and said, "We need to keep this between us until we know more. Are you okay with that?"

"Is it illegal, or just against policy?" Amanda asked.

"Maybe neither," Sofie said. "It's information about the crime, and it could solve the case, or it could be nothing. If it gets out, there will be problems. Not just for us. The whole station will be affected."

"It sounds too interesting to say no. I'm trusting your judgment, but only so far. If I think the captain needs to know, I'll tell him."

"You won't have to," Sofie said. She told Amanda what they'd found, and Rick placed the data film on the table.

33

"We're missing something," Amanda said. "It looks like a lot of information, and it is, but we're missing a link to turn it into real evidence."

Three hours of scanning documents, trying to pick out data points, looking for any clue leading to the identity of the partner had made all of them exhausted and bitchy. More worrying, Sofie's fingers were tingling. Not the regular slow rise from barely noticeable to just short of painful. An erratic stutter of sensation that she barely noticed before it was gone.

They were too close for her to drop another dose, and Rick already suspected she had a problem, so he might be on the alert.

"I need some air," Sofie said. "Let's take five minutes away. Maybe something will surface if we stop focusing so closely."

Rick stretched and rubbed the small of his back. "We need snacks. I'll go. A bit of a walk might help."

Amanda put her pad facedown on the table. "I'll come

with you. I don't trust you to bring anything with even a hint
of nutrition. We can't go all night anyway. We need sleep.
We need a fresh perspective, maybe let our subconscious
work on the problem for a while."

They left Sofie before she could say anything more. She
slipped out of the room and headed for the toilets. Only a
few of the night shift officers were in the bullpen. They were
chatting and pretending to update records. Sofie remembered the luxury of wasting time. Only three days ago she
would have been doing the same with Rick.

In the toilet, she pulled out the pack of meds. They
couldn't be that weak. She was already taking three times
Bindes's recommendation. Maybe it wasn't the Fades; she
was overflowing with stim-juice. If it was the caffeine, she
could dilute the effect by drinking water. It would take
some time, but it would mean she didn't need to take even
more of the medication. There were side effects, after all.
Bindes warned her at the beginning of their relationship
and periodically reminded her that overdosing could
bring on an attack, or muddle her memory, or affect her
speech.

She leaned over the sink to get a look at her eyes. Blood-
shot. That didn't help her decide. Her hands weren't trembling, but that could start at any time. And if the tingles
were different from normal, could she risk having her hand
suddenly shake?

The risk of her symptoms giving her away was too high.
She took one med and swallowed it dry. Water from now on.
The case was so close to breaking, Sofie didn't want to risk
anything getting between her and the capture.

Back in the room, Sofie projected a list on the wall. The
information they needed to catch the killer, and what they'd
tried so far. Missing kids, missing parents, unidentified part-

ner, weapon. The motive was a guess but seemed solid. Either the partner gets greedy, or the parents get revenge.

"Shit, we don't have the weapon," Amanda said. "How could we miss that?"

Sofie checked the windows. Still on private mode. "Forensics should have something by now," she said.

Amanda tossed the snacks on the table and grabbed her pad. "Yes, it's here. Not the actual weapon, that's probably been recycled into a machine part by now. It was a dual-edged sharp instrument. No match to any tool on the manufacturing lists. About hand length, so easy to conceal. Only Sato's DNA found."

Rick opened the door and joined them. "What if we updated the timeline?"

Sofie watched him walk to the wall and run his finger along the current record. "We haven't done that since day one." She joined him. "It's going to get crowded if we add all the details."

Amanda started typing. "We'll extend it back a month. Add the missing kid dates. I don't have any information on Sato family activity back that far."

The timeline populated with the names of children. "How sure are we of the timing?" Sofie asked.

"The dates are right, but time of day we have no idea." Amanda kept adding information.

"Add the dates on the parents who are missing," Rick said. "They'll be less accurate, but who knows."

"Okay, that's all of it." Amanda joined them at the wall. "Anything jump out at you?"

"Two days," Sofie said. "The kids disappear and two days later the parents. And look. No kids after his murder."

The partner is waiting out the investigation. Sofie had no doubt that if they didn't find the people behind the disappearances, it would start up again within days of the murder case closing.

"We still don't have a way to connect the kids to Oswald," Rick said. "And if we only add those data points, we're not doing a good job. All we have here is the information that points to the parents. If the killer is the partner or someone else, we've got nothing but our instinct."

We aren't at that point yet, Sofie thought. Sure, we could say it was one of the parents, even find one of them to interrogate. In a regular murder, the case would be lost when the defense pointed out the bias. It was so obvious in this one, the judge might refuse to take the case. And this wasn't a regular murder. Sofie had the bad feeling that no judge would see the case regardless. That the suspect would disappear and never be found again.

"We need to know what was happening in the Sato family for the months before. Something got between Oswald and his partner. Even if the partner didn't murder him, or arrange the murder, something happened."

"Otherwise, he wouldn't have been in the dark streets alone," Rick said. "This has been going on a long time. There's got to be an agent in Maintenance doing the actual kidnapping. For some reason, Oswald came into the dark streets to handle something himself."

"I think we finally have something to go on," Sofie said. "Yesterday I would have picked Mitch as the agent. But I don't think anyone would trust him with something this dirty. He crumbled too fast."

"The Elites have official people to do their work," Amanda said. "Maybe not murder, but anything that deals with the lower levels."

"Not the Seconds," Rick said. "The Executive liaisons, and most of the Prathams have Elite aides."

"Any of them disappeared?" Sofie didn't believe someone like Nhu or Haadiya would kill or be involved in selling kids. But they weren't the only liaisons. Nhu would know about the Ruiz family issues and the rumors on the rest. Haadiya would know the same about the Sato family. Maybe if they both reported the same rumors, it would lead somewhere. "We need more before we talk to our sources. Whatever we ask will be in the ear of an Elite within minutes."

Amanda searched the database. It only took seconds for her to say, "Nothing."

34

F rustrated, Sofie grasped for another question. One that might lead the investigation more than one step forward before it hit a dead end. "Do we know who Oswald Sato's aide was? Would anyone notice if he or she was missing?"

Amanda slid her finger across her pad. "No listing, but I'm not surprised. People will be trying to distance themselves from whatever stink is coming since we found the kill site."

Every step forward in an investigation brings its own baggage, Sofie thought. "Do we have access to any of the Executive or Elite databases?"

No one was immune from having their movements and correspondence tracked. The higher levels were given the right to restrict access to the records, but the records were there.

Amanda shook her head. "Access to anything we need only includes the lower levels. I guess no one official wants to be caught thinking an Executive or Elite is capable of committing crimes."

"Know anyone who can hack in?" Rick asked. "I don't think we'll get in through the official channels."

"Before we commit our own crimes," Sofie said, "are there any missing people in the levels we can search? Administration? Judges? Support? Oswald might not want his aide in possession of information that could be used against him. An accomplice from outside the family might be easier to manipulate. One inside, even an aide, might have ambition, and that could result in betrayal."

"And you have two people who would know," Amanda said as she searched databases. "Nhu and Haadiya."

Sofie's first reaction was to say no. She tried to think why that was. Did she think either of them was involved? No. She trusted Nhu. Haadiya was another matter.

"Nothing useful in Support," Amanda said. "One of the head administrators is off-station, has been since well before the crime. Two judges passed away and haven't been replaced."

"Natural causes?" Rick asked.

"They were ten years past the average age expectancy for their position. Nothing in the autopsies. You should talk to your contacts."

"I'll get Haadiya in the morning," Rick said. "He'll be more pleasant if I don't wake him in the middle of the night shift."

"You sure we can rely on his information?" Sofie asked. "Or on his discretion?"

"Yes. If I make it clear there's an advantage in it for him. I'll think of something. Why don't you trust him — no, that's the wrong question. Why do you trust Nhu more? What is it about Haadiya that makes him the bad guy?"

"Nhu has never asked for quid pro quo," Sofie said. "They are open about keeping stuff from me when it's not to their benefit. Look, I know that we can't really trust anyone from the Executive or Elites. We can't trust anyone from any level during an investigation, particularly one this high profile. But Haadiya Rothwell gives me the creeps. He's never volunteered anything."

She wasn't sure where the rant came from. She was tired, but did the meds take away her caution? Voicing her feelings didn't change anything.

Amanda ignored them to focus on her pad. She didn't have a source to protect. The thought pulled Sofie's mind from defending Nhu. There was no way she didn't have a source. She just kept the name under wraps. In fact, Nhu and Haadiya were the only sources who felt safe coming into the bullpen. Neither of them cared if they were identified.

Sofie held up her hand to break the pattern of accusations. "They are both playing two games — at least two. Someone lets them come to us publicly. We don't know how many half-truths they've knowingly given us. Or what they've reported back on us."

"Good to know you've caught up to the rest of us," Rick said.

"It's not news. I always check Nhu's information, and I never give them more than I should in trade. We need a plan."

"Talk to them both," Amanda said. "Compare stories and work with what you think is the most true."

"What about hacking the Elite and Executive databases?" Sofie asked. "Just in case we need to do it."

"I have someone I can ask. Just remember, if we can get a hacker to break in, anyone can. You can't completely trust the results. You want me to reach out?"

It would be better not to get caught digging through the lives of the people who ran the Mallet. "Wait until we talk to our sources," Sofie said. "Is there anything we can look at?"

Amanda flicked her pad and projected a list of public financial records. "I'm sure the information is properly sanitized," she said. "You aren't going to find a line item for assassins. But maybe I can check the income and expenses over the last week. What's not there might help us more than what is."

"You should transfer to Intelligence Squad," Sofie said.

Amanda turned off the projection. "How do you know I'm not from there?"

Sofie laughed. "I can only juggle so many conspiracies at a time."

"Tomorrow?" Rick asked. "Or now?"

Taking time out to rest could bring the momentum to a grinding halt. The same for their talk with Nhu and Haadiya. "It's probably going to be short," Sofie said. "Amanda, take off when you need to. Rick and I will update you with the results."

Amanda didn't look up from her pad. The woman could go forever when she had juicy data to feed her. "Let's get meetings set up. We can come back here to debrief. I hope to all the order in the universe we get a lead."

"Haadiya is up," Rick said. "Meeting him at his favorite bar. I'll reach out when we're done." He hustled through the bullpen without another word.

Sofie sent a request to meet with Nhu. The response came in seconds.

We have ten minutes. Come to our meeting space.

Too easy. Was Nhu waiting for her call? If Nhu and Haadiya were colluding, this was going to be a waste of time, and they were not going to be given an unlimited number of days to catch the killer of a Pratham. Sofie expected to be given a scapegoat in the next day or so.

35

Nhu's meeting space was different from June Sato's. The walls were patterned as if someone had painted a mural on them. There was no desk. A comfortable chair sat across a coffee table from Sofie, and the floor looked like it was grass, something she'd heard of but never seen. She hadn't expected this touch of warmth from Nhu, but perhaps like the jewelry and clothing, this indicated their preferred gender for the day.

The decor didn't make her feel comfortable, as she expected was the intent. It reminded her how odd it was that this was the first time she had met Nhu here. Maybe Nhu came to the bullpen not because they felt safe, but because nothing would be recorded. Every meeting in a virtual space was recorded and stored. Accessing the audio recordings required a high level of authorization. An Executive could control that access, but perhaps too many others could too.

"What did you wish to talk about?" Nhu's voice pulled Sofie back to the present. "We have meetings to attend before we can return to our quarters for rest. This murder is causing havoc, and not simply for the Sato family."

"I hope the Ruiz family is not too inconvenienced," Sofie said. "We are close to finding the culprit, I assure you."

Nhu nodded and sat, hands in their lap, waiting.

"You are aware that the Sato Pratham was murdered in the dark streets?"

Nhu nodded again. They were not usually this unwilling to engage in conversation. There was definitely something holding them back.

"We would like to speak to his aide." Sofie chose not to start a question about missing Elites or Executives. If Nhu felt the need to be cagey, Sofie could follow their lead. "We have been unable to find out who that was in our records."

"You should ask Haadiya Rothwell."

"We are," Sofie said. "It would be a mistake to rely on his information only, I'm sure you agree."

That brought a smile to Nhu's face. "It is a skill to know what you can trust individuals with, yes. We have heard the aide went missing recently. Tran Gilbride. It would be a mistake to think Tran is guilty of this crime."

Sofie didn't miss the hint that Tran could be guilty of any other crime. "I'm sure finding a valuable member of the Sato staff would be seen as a priority."

"Your murderer has nothing to do with any Elite family, Sofie. Please do not destroy your very promising career by even thinking you might find your killer here."

"Thank you for your concern about my future. I am sure Haadiya Rothwell will provide any relevant details."

"Tran Gilbride is likely in hiding until the new Pratham is elected. No one wishes to be purged from their job." Nhu glanced at the wall behind Sofie. "We must leave you."

"One more question?"

"Very well," Nhu said, standing. They flicked a finger and the decor disappeared, leaving a gray blankness.

"Is there a chance we can get authorization to review the entries for the Pratham and this Gilbride? Knowing the details of the Pratham's last days might provide some direction."

"Ex-Pratham," Nhu said. "We cannot provide any access to information on Elites or Prathams, and we suggest you think carefully about asking through official channels. We did warn you about looking in the wrong places to solve your case." Nhu flicked their fingers again and disappeared from the image.

WHEN SHE RETURNED the case room, Sofie was not surprised to find Amanda alone. Hopefully Rick had more luck with his contact. As much as Haadiya gave her the creeps, she couldn't imagine him acting like Nhu had. Sofie was still running the interaction through her mind. Nhu might not be chatty, but they had never treated her like a servant, and it set Sofie's instincts buzzing rather than upsetting her. And, surely, the Ruiz family shouldn't care enough about the investigation to order Nhu to freeze her out.

"Any joy in the financials?" she asked Amanda.

"Too soon to be sure. And I'm struggling to think. Time for that nap." Amanda stretched and turned the screen off. "Anything from Nhu?"

"I got a name and a warning. I think it might be too risky to hack into the databases."

"We'll see. Maybe Rick had better luck." She tipped her chin toward the bullpen.

Rick pushed open the door and dropped into the nearest chair.

"So?" Sofie asked. "What did you get?"

"The aide's name, and that he's missing. Denied access to the databases."

"Same here," Sofie said. "Tran Gilbride, right?"

"Yeah, so probably true. Haadiya thinks the guy is secretly lobbying for one of the candidates. I can find him tomorrow."

"Nhu thought he was hiding out until after the election," Sofie said. "Anything else?"

"He thought Oswald's partner was in the Temporaries. We should go talk to your contact." Rick checked his stim-juice glass but found it empty. "Tomorrow."

Torque wouldn't like it, but Sofie agreed. "Nhu was distant. I got the feeling they were hiding something against their better judgment. Why would the Ruiz family care?"

"Maybe we should have looked there before now," Rick said. "Their Pratham was interested at the beginning of the case, remember? Before the rest of them reached out to Llewelyn."

"Did you get warned off?" Sofie asked. "Like your career was on the line if you looked too high up in the Mallet for answers?"

"Now that is interesting," Rick said. "Amanda, can you get the Ruiz financial papers?"

"The public ones only," Amanda said. "I can look for patterns between them, but public records are cleaned."

Sofie's exhaustion was growing. This was important, but they couldn't afford to miss something because they needed sleep, or misinterpret something for the same reason. "Tomorrow at four hours. Rick and I will head into the Temporaries. Amanda, you can send us anything you find."

Sofie watched the others leave and checked that everything was shut down or locked away. She set the windows on permanent privacy, then set a tiny camera to record any activity while they were gone. It might be tiredness, but Nhu's warnings had Sofie on high alert. She tested that the door was locked before walking out of the bullpen, the stim-juice and meds overload warring with her body's demand for sleep. She had sedatives at home, but Bindes had warned against that. Only this one time, she promised herself.

36

As Sofie and Rick walked through the Maintenance section, people turned their heads to follow them. The section was always noisy with arguments verging on fights, raucous parties and celebrations spilling out of pubs and restaurants, and people hurrying between work and home. Today it was quiet. Not the peaceful kind; a menacing silence that seemed ready to boil over with the slightest provocation. Like the side-glances she noticed from people as they walked past. No words, but definitely a challenge. And again, there seemed to be more people than usual hanging around.

"Did something happen last night?" Sofie asked Rick.

Rick checked the news on his pad as they continued through the corridors. "Some idiot in the media is trying to blame Maintenance for the spike in violence."

"Fuck," Sofie said. She'd been expecting something like this. The Mallet media didn't care about repercussion, just followers and ad sales. "Did they give any details?"

"Of course not." Rick glanced around and walked closer to Sofie. "Why give facts when innuendo is easier and more fun? I guess it's a good thing they haven't named a suspect. We probably need to let Mitch go soon."

Sofie wished she could say they only needed to concentrate on the case, but she didn't have to strain her imagination to know what would happen next. "Have they suggested that no one is safe if a Pratham can be killed in public?"

"Not yet, but... well, that wouldn't be wrong." Rick shut down the news feed and dropped his pad into his jacket pocket. "I'm sure Llewelyn will be putting on the pressure to keep things from boiling over."

The entrance to the Temporaries was empty. "It looks like no one wants to be around if things kick off," Sofie muttered. "Let's find Torque. Let me do the talking, and if he says you should leave, just go."

Ten minutes later they sat at a table in Torque's favorite restaurant and waited for the mech to deliver drinks. Water for Sofie, but the two men chose weak beer. She shuddered at the idea of alcohol this early, but weak beer was no worse than stim-juice.

"You have someone in custody?" Torque asked as their drinks arrived. "What do you want from me?"

"Don't sulk, Torque," Sofie said. "I needed my partner with me. He won't bother you."

"He's welcome to bother me when he's off duty," Torque said. "Now, I'm busy, so let's get to it."

Sofie told him the high points of their progress, although there were too few for the investigation to be called anything other than stalled. "We need to find the parents. And Oswald's partner." She trusted Torque further than most people, but it made sense to her to keep their actual progress under wraps. Maybe Torque would add something they didn't know if he thought they were unaware of the details.

"I never saw the Pratham with a companion," Torque said. "I'm sure you realize that a partner would have to be a high-level Elite."

She'd been hoping for a name, one to confirm their suspicions. "Another Pratham?" He didn't know they'd already learned that fact.

"Any kids missing in the last few days?" Torque asked.

"Not yet," Rick said. He swirled the half glass of beer before looking at Torque. "Probably waiting until we catch the killer."

"So to save kids you could just let the case die out," Torque said.

Sofie could feel the jitters returning. She'd burned off most of the jumpiness from too much stim-juice during her sleep. Not all of it, but enough that she could tell the difference between the onset of an attack and simple jitters.

Sitting and talking was not helping, but this was their only choice. "The Elites will find a scapegoat," she said. "This won't end up an unsolved. We need information to get the right person, even if it's a parent."

"So, you'd punish a grieving mother for stopping that awful business? I thought you had a heart, Sofie."

Torque was just marking time. He knew something, Sofie was confident. "We don't punish. That's for the judges."

"Yeah, yeah. You just feed the machine," Torque said. "You know if this was somewhere off the Mallet, Oswald would be locked up. You'd have the partner's name and most of those kids would still be running around."

"Well, we are on the Mallet. And there are plenty of worse places." Sofie finished her water and pushed the glass to the center of the table. Time to give Torque something to deny, even if she wasn't convinced herself. "We figure a parent killed Oswald. The only place they could disappear is in your section. You're planning to smuggle them off-station, right?"

"So blunt." Torque leaned in and dropped his voice. "You have no proof that it was a mother or father. You won't get to search my area without pissing off a lot of important people. And even if you're right, could you bring yourself to take in someone who cleaned up that kind of shit?"

He might not know who the partner was, but his words confirmed for Sofie that the missing parents were hidden somewhere in the Temporaries, waiting for space on an outgoing transport so they could disappear into the galaxy. "What about Tran Gilbride? Oswald's aide. He's missing."

"You should look at the remaining Prathams if you want to find Gilbride. They tend to steal staff from each other just for sport. Or any of the Sato candidates. Yes, Gilbride would know everything. He's not in my section. I would know."

"I get it," Rick said. "You have some kind of hero complex. Saving the poor, oppressed Mallet workers. Have you been outside your section lately?"

Torque shrugged, but Sofie could tell he knew what Rick was insinuating.

"Nothing out there is of interest to me. If you refer to the muttering and glaring? Well, if it gets bad enough, we have a way out. We follow the rules. We care about the business arrangements that keep the Mallet running and the people fed."

Rick glanced to the street and then back. "If it escalates, you must know a mob doesn't care. They run on fury and spite. The line on the floor marking the border of the Temporaries isn't a wall."

Before Torque could respond, Sofie added, "It's pretty

quiet in here today. People trying to hide from what's coming?"

"I'll ask around discreetly about your parents and Tran. But I don't know the name of the partner for certain." Torque raised his hand to call the mech over. "People at this end of the Mallet have been unhappy for a long time. Finding the killer might calm things or be just the flame that ignites rioting. Tread carefully, Sofie."

She stood and gestured for Rick to do the same. "Tell me as soon as you have information."

Torque ordered another drink and pretended to ignore her words.

Out in the street, the residents of the Temporaries were stirring, but the few parties were subdued and none of them moved near the entrance to the section.

"He's right," Rick said. "If a riot is coming, we might not be able to stop it."

"We just do our job," Sofie said. "We solve the case. We don't decide the outcomes."

"Maybe that's true, but I would prefer not to be a scape-goat for the fall of the Mallet."

Sofie elbowed him. "Don't be so dramatic. Anyway, Torque will tell me about the parents. I know him too well for him to hide a lie. He knows where the parents are, and he knows exactly who the partner is. Maybe I should have come alone. Maybe he didn't like you being there."

"Yeah, a Pratham makes sense. Unfortunately, six of them have been poking into the investigation, and if we try to investigate one Pratham, we'll be standing on a Manufac-turing line by the end of the hour."

37

S ofie and Rick sat at a table in the back of a small bistro in the Temporaries section and ordered stim-juice and pastries. Sofie checked her notes and entered the comm code Lilianna Ruiz gave her. Maybe following up on the offer to help would reveal a clue to the name of the partner, even if it was Ruiz herself. She expected an automated appointment bot, but Ruiz answered after one tone.

"Yes, Detective?" The Pratham did a great job of projecting a desire to help in her tone, while being clear that she was busy.

"Pratham, I apologize for the disturbance. We received some... delicate information that you might be able to clear up for us."

"If I can, of course. This murder is upsetting to all the Prathams."

She doesn't know about the growing unrest, or she doesn't care. "We have reason to believe that ex-Pratham Sato worked with another high-ranking individual. One outside the Sato family."

Lilianna's attention snapped into focus. "Do you have a name?"

"No, unfortunately we were unable to glean that information from the available data. I thought you might have information we can't access about the business structures."

Sofie worried that if she asked a direction question Ruiz would end the call. And she wouldn't give the woman any names. She hoped Ruiz wouldn't suspect a source gave them the information. If the Pratham thought there was someone behind this who knew too much, Sofie wouldn't be able to protect anyone.

"I don't have dealings with the Sato family business," Ruiz said. "Our interests don't align in that way. Who gave you the information?"

"I can't reveal the names of our sources. I'm sure you understand the need to protect people who are brave enough to step forward and do the right thing."

"Are you saying I am not to be trusted?"

Sofie smiled to soften the words. Rick moved closer but stayed out of visual range. Sofie had hidden any location information before making the call. Ruiz wouldn't know they were in the Temporaries, let alone sitting in this specific bistro.

"Of course you are trustworthy," Sofie said. "If a detail of the case leaks out, I don't want you to be suspected. It helps to know that you and Oswald Sato didn't engage in business together. One more question, if you have another moment."

"Ask and we'll see if I have time to answer."

So much for giving us all the help we need. "Tran Gilbride, Oswald's assistant. Have you ever met him?"

Ruiz paused as if she was trying to sift through her memories. Sofie didn't buy the act. She was trying to decide how much of a lie she could get away with.

"Possibly at a meeting, or an event. I don't recall specifically. Why do you ask?"

"He, along with a number of people we'd like to question, has disappeared."

"I know nothing about people disappearing, Detective. My family does not condone criminal behavior. Is there anything else?"

"Thank you for your time, Pratham."

"You may speak to my representative in the future. If you have questions for me, Nhu Eckerman will relay them." Ruiz cut the call.

Rick pushed Sofie's drink and pastry toward her. "You'd think someone who made it to Pratham would be better at lying."

Sofie took a bite of the pastry. Butter and chocolate woke her appetite. The Temporaries got supplies from off-station. No resident would have access to ingredients this good.

"I don't think she's had experience lying to anyone outside her social caste. It's hard to be convincing when you don't have the right cues. I thought she gave it a good try. Or maybe she wanted us to think she was a bad liar."

Rick grunted agreement and finished his stim-juice. "Let's hope that doesn't change. I don't trust any Elite on principle, but if we can't tell when they're lying about something specific, we're screwed."

"Maybe she doesn't know anything. It's probably harder for her to admit she's ignorant of something than to lie about facts she knows."

"Even if that's true, we don't know what to do about it."

Sofie finished her pastry as she thought through the last hour. Lots of information but very light on details. She believed Torque when he said he didn't know the partner's name but had no doubt he was hiding the parents. Probably not Tran. Ruiz she didn't trust at all.

"You know, she was careful to say the families didn't work together," she said finally. "Maybe it was a personal gig. Something not official."

"Like a child kidnapping business?" Rick checked his pad. "We need hard evidence to accuse a Pratham of murder."

"She probably won't get charged," Sofie said. "But maybe the Ruiz family will want a Pratham who doesn't bring the cops to the door."

"So we dig deeper on Lilianna Ruiz? See if she makes a good suspect even if we can't arrest her?"

There was no one else to investigate. "Yes. Maybe we're wrong and you won't find anything." *Closing that avenue will help me feel better.*

Rick roared a laugh. "Sure. I have a contact I can use to get dirt."

"And I need to keep an eye on Torque." There was no way she could do that in secret. And hanging out in the Temporaries might give her a chance to look for the parents' hiding place. "Go ahead. I'll stick around here. Just check in periodically."

"Thanks. I hate this section. No one is actually in charge. At least the dark streets have someone to reign them in." He walked out of the bistro, leaving Sofie to ponder her next move.

The one good thing about no one being in charge of the Temporaries was that no one had the authority to kick her out. She paid the bill and strolled out to the street thinking about where she would hide a group of fugitives. Close to the launch bays for sure.

38

The outgoing shuttles were launched from a series of bays that crossed the back end of the Mallet. Three hundred shuttles headed out loaded with processed ore, manufactured items, and people six times a shift. No one was authorized to be on those ships except envoys from the Mallet and Temporaries who were returning home. People who paid to escape the hell of their lives in the lower castes, or to dodge retribution from crime bosses, neighbors, or the authorities went as cargo.

Everyone knew it happened, but no one bothered to look into it. Or maybe they tried without success enough times to give up.

Torque had to be part of the smuggling operations, but he wouldn't give Sofie any details about his business at all. Her search was based on guesses and a little knowledge of the setup. There was order to the launches. If someone was escaping, they would look for a safe haven. Some of the shuttles traveled between stations like the Mallet. Some went to planets, and some supplied long-distance colony ships.

Sofie headed for the bays that serviced planets. That's where she would go if she needed to escape, and if she didn't have the Fades. A condition unique to the Mallet made it very difficult to change identities somewhere else.

The section was laid out the same as the rest of the non-Elite parts of the station. Straight passageways made to look like streets were interrupted by the occasional open square with restaurants, stim-juice bars, and retail outlets. The residential areas were clean and well lit, the units twice the size of any in the Maintenance or Administration sections. The mechs were kept serviced, and within an hour any detritus from the frequent public parties was gone.

In the shuttle bays, gray-overall-clad workers hurried between storage areas and waiting shuttles. They crossed paths without touching at a pace that should have resulted in multiple collisions.

Could the storage spaces contain people waiting to be loaded? Not in the open, she thought. There would be containers fitted with tight living spaces. With environmental equipment and food for the journey.

She slipped through the opening and hugged the outside wall to avoid disrupting the traffic flow — and getting caught. She trusted that the people in the bay would be too focused on their tasks to notice her.

The first storage area was actually the end of a large conveyor. Open containers of ore moved to the end of the belt where an inspector scanned the contents before a lid was attached.

No one would be using those crates for smuggling people because it meant sure death.

She pulled out her pad and held it in front of her as though checking a manifest or some other document.

People were crossing the delivery area opening without

a problem. She observed until she felt comfortable. Ten steps and then stop for a container to pass. Walk fast across the gap and then you were clear.

The next bay was storage, but the packages were too small to hold a fugitive. She lingered at the entrance to make sure there were no hidden spaces where people could wait for a ship. A mech moved stacks of small boxes into larger crates. Those crates were transported to a waiting shuttle.

From her position beside the entrance, Sofie had a better view of the bay. The coordinated movements looked like a ballet from her new angle. The paths crossed and people, equipment, and mechs passed without a hitch — the humans didn't even look up from their tasks. The smooth flow highlighted the anomalies at the edges. Sofie wasn't the only one moving around the perimeter. Some stepped out to join a path, probably people reporting for work. Some did the opposite, stepping from a path to the perimeter, ending a shift. One storage area was different. Instead of workers entering a storage bay empty-handed and exiting with a mech or hand-driven forklift, some of the workers entered with small boxes and left empty-handed.

No one needed to place items in a storage bay from this side. They were all supplied from the Manufacturing section through the back of the area.

She'd found the parents.

Sofie checked the traffic in front of her and stepped out.

A hand grabbed her elbow and pulled her into the storage area. Someone sprayed her face with a blinding agent that burned her eyes, and then they pushed her hard. She bounced off a corner or a doorway and slammed into a wall. A door clicked and the buzz of activity outside was silenced. No sound of breathing other than her own gulps of air.

The blinding agent dried into a film that only blurred her vision. Sofie reached up to feel the edges of it and started to rub. The film lifted in moments. It didn't help her see because there was no light inside the space. She stretched her arms to find the limits of the room. Her fingertips brushed the wall in both directions. Yes, she was alone. She'd been pushed straight in, so she was at the back of the room. Moving her hands in front of her, she stepped forward. Two steps to the door.

Her fingers started trembling. *Fuck*. Now was not the time for an attack. Sofie fumbled for the pack of meds. Only five left. She swallowed two and waited, panic already building as the pack fell from her fingertips. If she had an attack now, how would she escape? She couldn't force her brain to calm enough to make a plan. She couldn't afford to have Rick know her secret, but she pulled out her pad so that she could call for help if things got that bad.

The pad added a glow to the darkness.

No signal.

39

S ofie slid down the wall to sit. Her brain was spiraling deeper into panic as the symptoms increased in intensity. Was someone waiting outside for her to black out? Did they know about the Fades? She needed calm to give the meds time to work. Adrenalin would only magnify the attack. She held her breath to break the gasps that were doing nothing but spiking her heart rate. *Breathe. Breathe. Breathe.* She added a count of five between the words.

If someone was coming to let her out, Sofie wanted to be standing and ready to fight. Her fingers were shaking now. Her thoughts seemed clear, but if she was already in the middle of an attack, would she know? Was the blackout just erasing her memory? Had she asked these questions before? She needed her hands steady to escape. Her pad was still giving her enough light to see the three doses held tightly in the blister pack she'd dropped. She forced her right hand to reach for the meds. It took time to convince her hand to close around the package. She would never get it back to her lap and convince the other hand to pop the doses out.

Her vision blurred and then cleared. The pills were scattered on the floor. How long? She didn't have the concentration to check the time on her pad, every ounce of control she still had over her body focused on the pills. She watched her hand pick up two of the closest, like someone was manipulating her arm. The final pill had rolled too far for her to reach.

Everything went dark. Then the light from her pad glowed. The pills were in her mouth. Sofie swallowed. Then her vision blurred and didn't clear. She told her brain to close her eyes, but nothing happened.

SOFIE WOKE WITH A JERK. How did she get here? The room was small and the only light was coming from her pad. A closet? She checked the time. Two hours since she'd met with Torque. That thought brought a rush of memories. Someone had locked her in this closet, jammed the network signal, and she'd had an attack. The meds had staved off the worst of it. Rick wouldn't be searching the station for her yet.

She pushed her body up the wall until she was standing. Granted, she was more *leaning* against the wall, but the weakness would fade, or she could ignore it. Fighting the urge to take the last pill, Sofie rubbed her hands together to increase her circulation. They shook too badly to continue, so she clasped them together and blew warm air across her knuckles. It felt like hours, but her pad said five minutes had passed when her hands steadied.

She waited two more minutes for all the after-tremors to settle, then stretched her hand out and touched the door. She moved to lean against it and listen for any sign someone was guarding her or coming back. Silence. She ran her fingers around the seam but couldn't locate a lock.

Closing her eyes, she leaned her forehead against the door and counted to ten as she tried to remember more details. Nothing. She straightened and looked around. She confirmed it was probably a mech closet. So the lock should respond to her authorization. She reached for the card and held it against the spot where a scanner should be. Nothing happened. "No signal, idiot."

Sofie didn't have a way to reverse a jammer. The police had tools, but they were all back in the bullpen. Unless her captors came back soon, she'd be dead before Rick or anyone found her — no food, only one pill, no water. The room wasn't completely sealed, but close enough. It meant the air wouldn't stay fresh for long and shouting for help was a waste of breath.

Maybe the people she was hunting were being relocated and the door would open soon because they no longer needed to keep her away. If not, one pill that didn't work as well as it should wouldn't stop the next attack.

"Why would they want me dead?" No. Not dead, unless they knew how bad her condition was. Delayed.

Time to stop worrying and find a way out.

She put her back against the rear wall and kicked at the door. It didn't break but did shift slightly from the force. Tracing the seam again showed a minuscule buckle where the lock should be.

Kicking the door open would bring too much attention, and maybe whoever locked the door on her had friends. Sofie moved to the back of the room and waited for someone to respond to the first kick. Three minutes passed and nothing.

She pulled out her stunner and turned the charge down. Shorting the lock wouldn't take much power or attract attention. She tested the point where the door buckled and placed the stun rods on the seam. Turning her face away and taking a deep breath, Sofie pressed the activator and held it.

The door popped just as she needed to take another breath. She eased it open and then gasped in clean air.

No one was in the bay. She slipped out and ran to the other side, tucking into the shadows as soon as she stopped. Too slow, but she couldn't push her body this soon after an attack.

Three breaths to steady herself and then Sofie looked around the doorway to the next storage bay. Everyone in sight was carrying out their tasks without looking around. She slipped around the divider and hid behind a stack of pallets to wait for the next person to deliver a package inside. She needed to see exactly what happened to avoid the risk of getting caught searching again.

Only a few minutes later, a female worker strode through the opening and past Sofie. She carried a crate and walked like she was just doing her job. Sofie tracked her to a large container halfway down the bay. The woman glanced back and then stepped around the rear. A couple of minutes later, she strode into sight, hands empty, and exited.

Sofie scanned the area to see if anyone was paying attention to the woman; no one was. She glanced into the open bay in case someone was making a second delivery.

She stepped out of the shadows and walked to the container. The loading gate was around the back. She held her ID to the scanner and the lock indicator turned green. The gate clicked open and swung away to reveal the interior.

Plastic crates were piled along the side, with a central path to the back. Four people turned to face her. The man signaled someone to stay hidden.

Holding up her hand for silence, Sofie stepped inside and pulled the gate closed. "I have some questions."

40

————

"Let us be," the man said, stepping toward Sofie.

He wasn't threatening, but Sofie held up her hand again to stop him advancing, knowing how quickly emotions could escalate. "Let's start with your names."

"Why should we tell you anything?" one of the women asked. "Who are you?"

Sofie pulled out her identification and held it so they could all see. "I know someone is hiding. Come out so I can see everyone."

Two more women and a boy joined them from behind a stack of crates. Sofie couldn't arrest them all. It wouldn't take much to overwhelm her while she recovered physically. These people were desperate enough to escape in a container to an unknown future. They could be capable of anything to hold onto that dream.

"I'm investigating a murder," she said. "I don't care about your plans. I think you have information to help me."

She recognized most of the faces from the missing persons reports: the Zim woman, the Lymans. The other woman was unfamiliar. She decided to pretend she didn't know them. If they gave different names, or if they admitted who they were, it meant something.

"I won't ask again for your names," she said. "Mine is Sofie Allen. I'm investigating the death of the Sato Pratham."

"We had nothing to do with it," Avi Lyman said. "We're doing nothing wrong. No rules against living here."

Only the last statement was the truth. They knew something about the murder. Maybe only the motive, or maybe they had killed him. She couldn't arrest them, because until they tried to leave the Mallet they were in the clear. Not showing up for work meant they didn't get money or food or shelter. Leaving the station was a whole slew of crimes.

"There's another man missing," she said. "Tran Gilbride. He was the Pratham's aide. I'm concerned that he is another victim. Or that he is the killer. Do you know him?"

The boy stepped forward. He was maybe ten, but Sofie could see his need to protect his family as he stepped away from the two women who reached to pull him back.

"We don't know anyone in the Elites," Lyman said. "We don't know about a murder. We can't help you."

As sad as their surroundings were, this was their home, and Sofie couldn't push for answers for fear of shutting them down completely. She could call Rick and bring everyone in for questioning, but she had nothing to connect them to the crime. And the entire group would be forced back to work, at worse jobs and with higher debt. She wasn't ready to do that.

"Okay. Let's talk about something different. I was attacked on my way here. Do you know anything about that?"

"It wasn't us," the boy shouted. "Leave us alone."

One of his mothers pulled him back. "He's scared. Please don't hurt us."

"Did you see who did it?" Sofie had no intention of hurting anyone. She was outnumbered and in close quarters and still weak. "If you can identify the person, you might not be safe here."

"We are safe enough," the man said. "We didn't see anything."

Another lie. "How often do you leave the container?"

"We leave to wash and take care of our needs." The answer came from Satareh Zim. The image from the missing persons report hadn't shown the pain in her eyes.

Satareh whispered something to Lyman. He looked like he wanted to argue but didn't. He went to the back to sit with the others. Satareh held some power in this group. Perhaps she had the contact for the smugglers.

"The boy saw," Satareh said. "He came back and told us. We didn't know what to do. You got out, so no harm done."

Not the truth, or not all of the truth. This woman was holding herself tightly, as if protecting the entire story. Sofie had the odd feeling she was bargaining for facts. "What did he see?"

"A man. Same clothes as the rest. He left when you were inside. The boy didn't see anything to help you catch your attacker."

None of that was true, but Sofie didn't want to get side-tracked. Finding the parents was only the first step. She wanted — no, needed — to know what had actually happened to get them to this point. And starting an official investigation of the person who locked her in the closet would reveal her condition.

When Sofie didn't speak, Satareh said, "You should leave us alone. We have done nothing wrong. You have a murderer to find. You have a missing Elite. Why waste time with us?"

"My job is to find a killer. How did you know to come here?" Sofie waved her arm to encompass the entire container. "People don't stumble on a place like this in the out-shuttle bay. Someone told you about it."

The woman smiled. "I will not betray that trust. Others may need a sanctuary."

Sofie ignored the smile. It was a ploy to include her in the poor, downtrodden victims that needed to hide. She had to separate Satareh from the group, take away her need to protect a little.

"Talk to me outside and I'll promise not to push any harder on these people. I need answers and you know the authorities won't ignore any lead in the death of a Pratham."

"And I will be able to return to my new family? You won't arrest me?" Satareh glanced back at the group, who were staring at them. "How do I know you can be trusted?"

She had something to say, or she'd just deny Sofie's request. Refusing would force Sofie to apply pressure or to drop it. She didn't want to do either, yet.

A reminder that she had backup might suffice. "I could have called in a squad to arrest you for something. You might not be doing anything illegal, but it won't matter unless someone challenges us."

"And that could be a long time from now, if ever," Satareh said, sighing. "Okay. Only outside our door. And only a few minutes."

She told the others not to worry and led the way outside. Sofie closed the door and checked to make sure no one was around. They had as much privacy as could be found in a busy section of the Mallet.

"What do you need to tell me?" she asked.

"You know about children going missing?"

Sofie nodded.

"I had two beautiful twins. One day they didn't come home. No matter what I did, I couldn't find any information. You cops didn't investigate. So I started watching. I saw our supervisor talking to the Sato Pratham. I heard Mitch talking to the Pratham's partner. A woman. An Elite I do not know."

"Mitch knew about the kidnappings?"

"I don't know how much. But he was working for the Pratham. I made a plan. I was going to get evidence for the police. I knew the Elites would be untouchable, but Mitch was supposed to protect us, not sell our children."

"You have the evidence?" The case could be closed in hours.

"Before I could get it, I saw something else." Satareh looked down at her hands. A sign of guilt? Regret? Fear?

"Tell me."

"That man you asked about, Tran Gilbride. He was arguing with the Sato Pratham. I didn't hear what it was about, but they entered a recess together, and the Pratham came out alone. When it was safe, I looked, thinking maybe the man needed a medic."

The pause was long enough for Sofie to prompt the woman. "And? Will I find Gilbride in a ward somewhere?"

"There was nothing."

"This was how long before the Pratham was murdered?" There might be a completely new motive.

"The day before. But by then I was already seeking a hiding place. If an Elite could be killed so casually, there was no hope for a grieving mother. When I found this place, I sent word to the Lymans, and they brought the other family."

Sofie believed everything Satareh said up to the last. She hadn't said anything about the murder, but she hadn't denied it either. She couldn't ask if she murdered Sato because Satareh would lie, but if she came at it from another angle, she might get the truth. "You do know who locked me in that closet."

Another look at her hands and then a deep sigh. "What will you do to this person?"

She wasn't ready to answer that question yet. If she laid charges, someone would eventually ask why she was taking up time on a minor charge. Sofie would ignore something so juvenile. "Probably nothing."

Satareh stared at Sofie as if she could read the truth in the words. "We can be moved, and I'm told we will be gone from this life soon. A new start on a new world. The boy. He only meant to delay you. When he finally returned to our hiding place, he told us. We would have freed you."

"I was attacked in the dark streets; you know anything about that?" It had to do with this case, but Sofie knew the attacker could have been paid by Oswald's partner. Or been a warning from the boss of the dark streets, despite the promise of safe passage.

"No. But the police don't do well in there alone."

"The Pratham?" Sofie left the accusation unspoken. Every instinct told her this woman only killed to protect others.

"If I tell you who ended that man's life," Satareh said, "will you let the others go?"

Not us. The others. Sofie needed to hear the answer. "I don't arrest people who are innocent."

"I killed him. I couldn't let him continue. I would have killed his partner if I knew who she was. But with Oswald

Sato and his aide dead, surely children would be safe for a while."

Sofie needed more than the confession. It wasn't recorded and there was no physical proof to tie her to the crime. "The weapon?"

"It is recycled." Satareh stared at Sofie. "Am I under arrest?"

Sofie could drag her off to face charges. She would be found guilty, not because of proof, because she was convenient. "When do you leave?"

"We don't know exactly, but not today."

"Go back to your friends," Sofie said with a nod to the container. "Don't bother hiding somewhere else. I'll find you."

41

No one paid attention to Sofie as she slipped out of the bay and through the streets to the Maintenance section. Knowing the killer's identity didn't settle her mind about the crime. What the Pratham did was horrible, but this was the Mallet, and horror was a way of life. Her cop instinct wanted her to find a reason to arrest the people in the container, even if it was just to make sure they didn't make it off-station before the case was closed. The rest of her hoped they were already in space. The death of a Pratham, no matter what he had done to deserve it, would mean retribution.

She found a stim-juice bar and took a stool so she could call Rick.

"Is Mitch still in custody?" she asked as soon as he picked up.

"Released an hour ago. Back to work, but under electronic observation. Why? You find something?"

Sofie trusted Rick to keep the location of the parents a secret, but she wasn't settled on her feelings about the situation. She wanted to be sure of her allegiance before she told anyone. Until now, she would have no doubts about her loyalty to the legal process, rather than what was, perhaps, more justice than legality. One of those sides would mean keeping quiet.

She stood and headed to Mitch's area. "A tip about our friend Mitch," she said. "He's involved and we need to find a way to prove it."

"I have something interesting on the Ruiz Pratham too," Rick said. "Mitch is hanging around the central offices. Meet you in fifteen?"

The central offices were responsible for work assignments. Mitch had every reason to be there, but Sofie couldn't stop the suspicion that he was up to something. "I can make that."

RICK WALKED UP to the entrance of the Maintenance central offices moments after Sofie. She could see Mitch inside, sitting on a chair, waiting for someone. Maybe he was getting reassigned or demoted.

"What do you have on Lilianna Ruiz?" Sofie asked.

"Nothing we can use against her officially," Rick said. "But I decided to get the hack into the Elite database. She talked to Oswald Sato multiple times in the months leading up to the murder. Five times on the day of. She has suspicious financial transactions that don't hit the family records."

"So we've probably found the partner." Sofie wished they could arrest an Elite but knew better than to waste her time. The woman wouldn't even be questioned. "Not a surprise really, but we won't be able to charge her. I guess we drop it."

"What did you get?" Rick kept his eye on Mitch. "Do we need to take him in or can we question him here? Get him in more trouble."

Sofie told Rick what Satareh said without giving away her identity or location. She wasn't ready to put his career on the line with the knowledge or trust him completely with her own fate. "I guess we won't find Tran Gilbride, and if no one reports him missing, we have no case to work. I say we talk to Mitch in a room here. Take him in only if we get something to charge him on."

Rick followed her through the door and went to the counter to demand a private room while Sofie approached Mitch.

"I've already told you everything," he said. "You know where I've been since I got out. I have nothing more to say."

She gestured for him to stand. "We have some questions anyway. My partner has a room for us here. Go through to the back."

Mitch didn't move. "Why? What questions do you have?" He kept his voice low, but Sofie figured he'd try to create a scene soon.

Sofie pointed to where Rick waited on the other side of the counter. "You'll find out when we ask. Move."

He glanced at Rick and then back to her before marching over to the man behind the counter. "Record when I go in and if I'm not out in ten minutes, come and get me."

The man took one look at Sofie and made a note. "I ain't your counsel. You get in trouble, you get yourself out."

The room was only big enough for two people to fit comfortably. Rick walked to the far corner and stood, arms crossed and looming. Sofie pointed Mitch to the chair facing the door across the narrow desk. She sat between

Mitch and the door. He was going nowhere until she was satisfied.

"What do you know about Tran Gilbride?" Sofie asked.

"Should I know something?" Mitch crossed his arms and leaned back smiling, until he bumped into Rick. "Who is he or she?"

"You were seen talking to the Sato Pratham before he was murdered," Sofie said. Making a statement sometimes triggered a usable response from a suspect.

Not this time. Mitch waited for a question.

"You were also overheard speaking to another Elite. Someone working with Oswald Sato in a criminal enterprise."

Mitch stopped smiling, but still didn't speak.

"Who was that person?" Sofie asked.

"Who told you I was talking to an Elite or two? No crime there anyway."

"Tran Gilbride disappeared, presumed killed, the day before the Pratham's murder."

"Told you I don't know anything about that."

"We are arresting you for abetting the murder of Pratham Sato and the disappearance of Tran Gilbride, his aide." It wouldn't stick unless they found proof, but Mitch would be in custody while they followed up on the details. She didn't hold out any hope that the comm calls Rick's hacker had found would be recorded. The Elite would have made sure of that.

"You can't arrest me for this," Mitch said. "I go down for something an Elite did, you will have riots. People have had enough of this shit. One rule for everyone else and no rules for the Elites. It'll blow up in your faces. Besides, I'd never sell kids off-station as cheap labor for the mines."

"Is that why he was getting you to steal them?" Sofie asked.

"And sex, and experiments, and any shit someone wanted to do to them and could pay for." Mitch didn't sound disgusted at all.

Sofie swallowed the bile in her throat.

Rick took a half step out of the corner. "You aren't that well-liked, Mitch. All that shit about people rising up in your defense. You think they'll do that when we explain you've been stealing kids?" He took Mitch's arm to pull him up.

Mitch shook off Rick's hand. "What if I talked?"

"I thought you didn't know anything." Sofie tapped the arrest order on her pad, not looking at him.

"Oswald stuffed that Tran guy down a recycler. He was alive."

Sofie looked up. How deep was Mitch in this scheme? They might not be able to go after the Ruiz Pratham, but Mitch didn't know they'd already identified her. "Who is the partner?"

"They'll kill me," Mitch whispered. "They'll manufacture evidence and I'll be convicted. I don't want to be the scapegoat."

"Tell us what you know, and we'll make sure that doesn't happen," Sofie said. "If they are looking to pin it on someone, we'll make it too hard for them to pick you."

"In writing," Mitch said. "I don't tell you anything until I have a deal. I want to get off-station."

"You'll be safer in a cell until we get someone who has the power to make the deal," Sofie said. "I've called for officers to escort you to the jail."

The escort arrived quickly and took Mitch into custody.

Sofie didn't think he'd get his deal, but she'd try. "A drink?" she asked Rick.

"Open Pit?" Rick asked in response. "You have to tell me the full story; it might as well be over a beer."

A beer was a good idea. Sofie knew how she wanted the case to end, and if Rick was relaxed, it would be easier to get him on her side.

42

M itch's comments about unrest came back to Sofie as they walked to the Open Pit. The mood of the crowds moving through Maintenance still didn't feel any different than normal. She might be fooling herself because it wasn't just Mitch pointing it out. But a riot could kill everyone on the station. Would it get that bad?

She assessed the mood as she walked beside Rick. People glanced their way like usual, but had they always sneered before looking away? She looked again, hoping to confirm everything was normal, but most of the people were wearing small patches on their clothes. The word *enough* stamped or embroidered in blue in the center of an orange circle. Yes, something was different. But wearing patches wasn't a crime, and no one was trying to gather a crowd or preach a message of rebellion. So, today at least, no danger. And if her plan worked, maybe everything would go back to normal.

When they walked through the door, Sofie noted Dr.

Bindes at this usual table. He looked her way but showed no recognition. She would be back later to talk about the meds.

They took a booth for privacy and Rick ordered beer for himself, water for Sofie, and a tray of snacks. "Might as well eat now," he said. "We aren't going to get a break until this is solved, right?"

"Let's hope that's today," Sofie said.

Rick grunted his agreement.

The food and drinks arrived and Sofie pulled out her pad. "We should have invited Amanda," she said. "Call her and see if she can get here fast."

"Afraid she'll be pissed if you make the call?" Rick laughed as he made contact.

"I can't get away right now," Amanda said. "Leave me on speaker so I know what's going on."

Sofie shook her head. She couldn't risk someone walking in on Amanda and catching even a little about her plan.

"I'll update you when I get back," Rick said. "What are you working on?"

"Reports. Llewelyn demanded written updates. Whatever you found, you opened a can of shit. I'll make sure these are all done before you get back."

Rick ended the call.

"You should get to know her more," he said. "She's a damn good investigator."

"And almost as good at stirring the pot." Sofie took a drink to give her time to pull her thoughts into some kind of order.

"We all cause trouble when we need to," Rick said. "So, did you solve the case?"

"This case can't be solved officially because too many important people are involved. But I think I've got it as far as we can."

She told him about the people in the container and what Satareh told her about Tran Gilbride — but not the confession. "So as far as I can tell, the Ruiz Pratham was the partner. Oswald was escalating the violence, and whoever killed him was taking revenge for his actions." She picked at the snack tray waiting for Rick's questions.

"I thought you weren't going to take risks without me again?" Rick said. He shook his head when she started to make excuses. "I was stupid to believe you meant it."

She hadn't gone into a risky situation purposefully, but she had gone alone. Rick's disappointment made her think about why. Because deep down she was terrified that he'd be there when an attack happened. "Sorry. I promise I'll try to be a better partner."

"Even if you could prove everything pointed to the Elites, they treat us all as objects to be exploited, so nothing would improve. The Elites won't change. Kidnapping kids might stop, but something else will pop up. So, you think Torque is helping get the people off-station?"

"Has to be, but I don't want to lose him as a contact for being a decent guy. From some things that happened, I have a feeling the boss of the dark streets is helping too, but I have even less to support that." *Mostly because if I told you he protected me when I was attacked, you would start asking questions I don't want to answer.*

Rick sat back, thinking. Sofie knew what she wanted to do, but maybe he had a better idea. Or if he wanted to go by the book, she needed to keep the plan secret.

"Look at it from a different angle," he finally said. "We need to solve the murder of an Elite. Not just an Elite, a Pratham. It was never going to be easy to prove and we've had almost four days to catch someone. The Elites are going to present their sacrificial lamb any moment."

"I want to control that." Sofie couldn't let the Elites define the outcome any more than they already had. If Mitch was right, the verdict could ignite riots.

"Two other crimes are being ignored," Rick said. "We're cops and we don't choose the assignments, and we know no one cares about the kids — except their parents. But Tran was an Elite. Why isn't anyone looking for him?"

"Because there are levels of value even at the top. None of us know how many low-ranking Elites disappear."

Rick was almost there. Sofie pulled on all her remaining patience to stop herself from blurting out her plan.

"That bastard got what he deserved," Rick said under his breath. "I know we don't want everyone taking vengeance, but there's no justice in putting any parent on trial for killing someone who sells kids."

"We need to pick the scapegoat," Sofie said. "I'm not sending someone to be punished for a crime they didn't commit, but we have some choices."

"Tran Gilbride?"

"Like you said, no one seems to care he's gone. I'll tell Torque to get those families off the Mallet as fast as possible. Can't have anyone tripping over them by accident. I'll make a good argument that Tran Gilbride killed Oswald Sato because he wanted a promotion, or was in a jealous fit or something. That he's gotten off-station."

Rick nodded and finished his beer. "Some of this needs to come from me or Amanda. It will be less suspicious if the team came to the same conclusion, not just you."

"I don't trust her," Sofie said. "I know you do, and I trust you. So you tell her what we need."

"I'll get her to plant a bit of proof in some files. What about the kids? If the Ruiz Pratham starts up again, we'll be right back here in a few months."

"Well, Haadiya and Nhu might come in handy to send a message." Sofie warmed at the idea of using them the way they used her. "Did we miss anything?"

"The boss of the dark streets? He might know the truth about who killed the Pratham."

"You know it's a man?" She did not relish contacting the boss. Even less giving him something to hold over her team.

"Yes, but I won't tell you how."

We all have secrets.

"He won't do anything to stop us, but if he tries to use the knowledge as leverage, I'll be the target. Let me figure it out." She hoped the boss wouldn't come after her.

"Let's get this done." Rick handed her the bill and stood. "I'll get Amanda onside and start the paperwork. Don't be long with your part, because Llewelyn will have questions."

She watched him stride out of the bar, paid the bill, and left for the Temporaries.

43

Torque was waiting for her when Sofie strolled into his favorite bar. She saw wariness in his eyes as she pulled a stool to the table and sat.

"We need to talk," she said. "You know why?"

He nodded and waited.

"Torque, you can't just be silent. I know you think you're safe because our laws don't apply here. You forget we can request your employer replace you on the Mallet."

He relaxed. Now that he knew what game she was playing, he knew what to do and say. Sofie waved away the server who approached. Torque might think he understood where the conversation was going, but she didn't want distractions. There was a small chance he wouldn't go along, and she didn't want to miss the clues.

"It might mean a better posting," he said.

In all likelihood, but the Mallet wasn't the worst place in the universe — just in the top ten. "I always wondered what you did to get this post. I mean, you're smart, and your morals are flexible. You could be on a pleasant world. Why here?"

He leaned forward, elbows on the table, and rubbed his temples. "I don't tell my story to anyone, Detective Allen. I thought we were friends, but if you're going to push the party line, I'll keep my mouth shut."

So, he was scared. "How many people have you smuggled out?"

"No comment."

"Did one of those parents kill the Pratham?" She figured he knew but wanted to hear him say it.

"No comment."

"Did you know about the kids all along?"

He flashed a glance around the room, then sat back. "No. Kids are off limits to the normal people in the universe. I found out too late to do anything about it. Including helping you like I've done in the past. You think I'd keep something like that to myself?"

"No, but I had to ask. Anyway, we're closing the murder case today," Sofie said. "Do you have anything to offer me? The documents aren't final yet."

He needed to make the offer to help. Until he did, Sofie was holding back. He was a key part of the plan, but those people were headed off-station regardless of what she did right now. For her plan to work, they had to be off the Mallet today.

"Maybe," he said. "Or maybe no comment. Who's getting blamed?"

"I have a list," Sofie said.

"Am I on it?"

Sofie stared at him. "No comment."

They sat in silence for a long moment.

"Okay," Torque said, breaking the standoff. "I'm an easy target. I get off-station and you accuse me. No one will come looking because the new Pratham will be in place, and everyone will move on."

"Do you know who killed him?" Sofie wanted her curiosity satisfied about how far Torque would go. It wouldn't change the plan because there would be no proof.

"Yes." Torque looked around again. Sofie followed his gaze. No one was nearby. Two tables at the front were occupied by large, strong-looking men and women. The bar staff were all on break together apparently. "What is your plan?"

Sofie told Torque his part. "If you can get them out by the end of today, you should be okay. It's best if you don't know anything else."

Torque pulled out his pad and tapped a message on the screen. "Two hours. Then they'll be beyond reach."

"Are they going to someplace better than this?"

"Low bar, Sofie. Yeah. They'll get jobs and a chance to start again. Maybe it will work out, but losing kids is hard to get over."

"You don't just smuggle people out and let them start over?"

"I'm just the man on the Mallet. So, yes. Our group wants our clients to succeed, and that means assistance after they arrive at their new home. That's all you need to know."

"The killer?" Sofie asked, wanting to be sure Torque was knowingly helping a murderer flee. It meant he could be trusted to keep her own willingness to do it a secret.

"The mother, but you know that. You talked to her. She had help but I don't know who it was, and I wouldn't tell you if I did."

She didn't want to know anyway. "Okay. You'll hear all about how Tran Gilbride lured Oswald Sato into the dark streets to kill him over a lover."

"Terrible what sex can do to a man's mind." Torque knocked on the table and the guards at the front moved away.

44

It had taken most of the night to craft the reports to close the case. Now, after a few hours of sleep, Sofie scanned the summary one more time. Amanda was checking on the data points she'd entered on the report to add veracity. Mostly facts she'd made up, and a few links she'd found in databases. Rick filed all the hard copies and evidence into storage capsules.

"I think it looks good," Sofie said. "A few details left unresolved makes it more real."

Amanda closed the screen of her pad and sat back to look at Sofie. "You know, I always thought you were a rule follower. I liked that you didn't have any political skills, but now? It feels like a real competition for the next promotion. You have taken a step down the dark road of compromise."

Sofie signed off the report and sent it to Llewelyn. "I have talents I keep to myself. But let me be clear: This is the right thing to do. This isn't the first step down a bad path. The rules are still what keeps us on the side of the good guys."

"Why don't you think *I'm* competition?" Rick asked. "I'm political. I'm a good cop."

Sofie and Amanda laughed.

"What?"

"You are, but you always end up in the wrong bed," Sofie said.

"True, I'm also an excellent lover." He closed the capsule. "Llewelyn took the news better than I expected. I think he was just hoping we'd come up with a believable result."

The meeting with the captain had been short and to the point. His concerns all related to how the story would play with the Elites. Sofie had no illusions about Llewelyn buying the answers. He didn't ask for details; he didn't want to know.

Nhu had been much the same when Sofie contacted them an hour ago. They accepted the answers and would advise the Ruiz Pratham to do the same. They hadn't argued when Sofie suggested that there were lines that shouldn't be crossed. That if children went missing again, the people of the Mallet would take action. Sofie didn't care that she'd used Mitch's tactic of threatening riots. She'd been more subtle than him and, hopefully, more effective.

The trick now was dealing with Haadiya. He was closer to the problem as the Sato liaison. Sofie wasn't completely sure how much he'd known about the business with the kids, or Tran Gilbride's murder, but she chose to make those things unimportant in her report so, with luck, he wouldn't ask any difficult questions about the result.

"He's here," Rick said, nodding toward the entrance to the bullpen.

Haadiya Rothwell, in a dark gray suit designed to high-light every attractive feature. If you didn't know he was a slimy, self-serving creep... but it only took a few minutes in his company to learn those things.

"Turn off the privacy," she said to Amanda. "Nothing here to hide anymore."

"Good morning. I understand you have a result." His bluntness was uncharacteristic.

Rick pushed away from the table and offered Haadiya a seat. "News travels fast between levels."

Haadiya smoothed his sleeves and declined the offer to sit. "News, yes. Not details. I forgive you for telling Eckerman first. The Sato family may not."

It wasn't her job to inform anyone but the captain. Procedure wouldn't be an excuse if the Satos chose to be offended. "I'm sure they were made aware through the proper channels."

"What do you know?" Rick asked. "I'd hate to waste your time with repetition."

"You have solved the case, you don't have anyone to charge with the crime," Haadiya said. "I need more for the new Pratham."

"So the election is done?" Sofie asked.

"You retain your position?" Amanda asked. "Isn't that unusual?"

Haadiya beamed. "I am unusual. My official role reports to the Second. That is still June Sato. I do a little work here and there directly for the Pratham. I hope to continue that."

Sofie didn't care who ran the Sato family now. She wanted them to accept the case was over and to stop stealing kids.

"We have no hard proof, but it seems that Tran Gilbride murdered Oswald Sato over some relationship. Maybe a shared lover, or maybe they were involved. We don't know for sure, and I don't think the Satos want us digging any deeper. It looks like Gilbride managed to buy his way off-station. No one else was involved, other than some paid dark streets thugs who moved the body."

"I see." Haadiya checked his jacket sleeves again. The man had no guile. "I think the Sato family will be satisfied. Do you know which business?"

Sofie looked at Rick, who said, "It wasn't official. I don't think the family will want the details published. I imagine the business has been shut down."

The room was silent as Haadiya digested the statement. Amanda started stacking the file capsules. Sofie noticed her attention was on Haadiya. Looking for a new contact in the upper levels?

"I see. Did this business leave any outstanding... debts?"

That was not how she'd refer to the parents who lost their children. And Mitch was demoted to work alongside the people he'd been exploiting with his petty schemes. Not really enough punishment for helping Oswald steal kids, but better than nothing.

"None," she said. "One small personnel issue that has been resolved. A good time to shutter and move on."

"Yes. The new Pratham will want to refresh the balance sheets and realign allies. I'm sure it will be months before anyone is assigned to delve into Oswald's private matters. Well, I must be off. You all look exhausted. I'm sure you would benefit from a few days off."

He walked out and through the bullpen without looking back.

"He likes to think he has more influence than he actually wields," Amanda said. "Something you can exploit."

Rick propped open the door so the mechs could access the records for storage. "He thinks he'll find a way to buy into the Elite. They'll never let him. And he isn't close enough to anyone to get leverage."

It did explain his behavior, Sofie thought. "He's right about time off. I'll clear it. Three days. Starting now."

She stood by the door and waited until they were out of the bullpen before stepping from the room. She needed a refill on her meds and then to sleep for two of those days.

45

D r. Bindes was at his usual place in booth when Sofie walked in. This time he was alone, so she didn't need to wait for a patient to leave.

"You looked happy yesterday," Bindes said.

Sofie ordered a beer; a little celebration was worth the risk of delaying sleep. "Solved the case."

"Why are you here, Sofie? Found a new lost soul to send me? Deacon is doing well, by the way."

Sofie sucked her lips in, suddenly afraid to speak. During the investigation, she only worried about getting through. Taking more than the maximum dose of meds seemed like a good idea. Now, she worried that she'd done more damage to her body. This case showed her how stupid her resistance to the operation was. She'd been taking risks simply to hide the possibility of discovery.

"Just tell me," Bindes said. "We'll figure it out. I have news too."

"What news?" Sofie felt like he'd thrown her a lifeline, not just a few moments before she'd have to admit she wasn't handling her condition.

"You first." He waved away the server and leaned toward her. "How bad can it be?"

"The meds aren't working as well as before. I don't know if it's my condition or something wrong with the dosage. I've had more attacks and less notice."

It sounded worse when she laid it out for him. There was more, but she needed his news before going any further.

"You saw your results. There is some deterioration, but the meds are a bigger problem," Bindes said. "You shouldn't have escalated so quickly because of that, but maybe the stress of the case?"

"Tell me about what you found. Are you sure you're safe?"

Bindes stood and beckoned her to his office. "This needs privacy. Bring your beer."

When they were settled, Bindes started testing Sofie's blood and reflexes. "Someone is diverting meds. I didn't find out where they are going. But the expiry date isn't right. Someone is tampering. Not just yours, either, although it's for more than just the Fades. I found ten other medications that didn't pass the test. They are all chronic-condition meds, and if this doesn't get fixed, people will die."

He checked the results of his tests while Sofie finished her beer. For her, there was a more permanent option — the operation — but for most people only medicine could keep them productive. Was someone just greedy, or was this an attempt to sabotage the Mallet? Without a productive workforce, the quotas would drop. Another station would take their business and the Mallet would die. No one would pay for the workers to be evacuated. The Elites would get out early, but everyone else would be left to a long, slow deterioration as food ran out and the basic law and order was overturned.

"How fast can you arrange for me to have the operation?"

"You'll need to be off-line for a few days. Rest is critical to recovery."

The time off wasn't a problem — unless the station erupted in riots. She hated the idea of being vulnerable on that table, not knowing if she was being cured or betrayed. She only had one person she trusted to watch over her while she was out.

"I want you in the room," she said. "Whatever it costs me, I want you there."

GRAB the next book in the series White Noise, here.

WANT MORE?

Is The Mallet safe? Use the QR code to White Noise and follow Sofie as she digs into a plot to destroy her home.

If you enjoyed reading Fade to Black, please consider helping other readers to find the story by leaving a review.

WANT MORE?

Is The Mallet safe? Use the QR code to White Noise and follow Sofie as she digs into a plot to destroy her home.

~

If you enjoyed reading Fade to Black, please consider helping other readers to find the story by leaving a review.

FREE EBOOK

Claim your copy of Running the Game when you use the QR code below to sign up for my newsletter and cheer on Pen as she vies for a commission in the military.

ALSO BY PA WILSON

For more books by P A Wilson

Use the QR code below or go to pawilson.ca

ABOUT THE AUTHOR

Perry Wilson is a Canadian author based in Vancouver, BC who has big ideas and an itch to tell stories. Having spent some time on university, a career, and life in general, she returned to writing in 2008 and hasn't looked back since (well, maybe a little, but only while parallel parking).

She is a member of the Vancouver Writers Social Group, The Royal City Literary Arts Society, and The Surrey Writing Workshop. Perry has self-published several novels. She writes the Madeline Journeys, a fantasy series about a high-powered lawyer who finds herself trapped in a magical world, the Quinn Larson Quests, which follows the adventures of a wizard named Quinn who must contend with volatile fae in the heart of Vancouver, and the Charity Deacon Investigations, a mystery thriller series about a private eye who tends to fall into serious trouble with her cases, and The Riverton Romances, a series based in a small town in Oregon, one of her favorite states. Her stand-alone novels are Breaking the Bonds, Closing the Circle, and The Dragon at The Edge of The Map.

For more information
www.pawilson.ca
pawilson@pawilson.ca

ACKNOWLEDGMENTS

People think that the process of writing is solitary. That's not the case for me. I have help from so many people it would be hard to acknowledge everyone, but I'll give it a try.

The support and inspiration I get from my writer's groups is incalculable. The Vancouver Writers Social Group opens my mind to other ways of telling a story. The Royal City Literary Arts Society gives me the opportunity to meet and share with other writers who have more knowledge than I do. The Other 11 Months group is where I learn about getting the words on the page. And my critique group who helps me find the best parts of the story I want to tell. Thanks to all of the members of these great groups.

Last of all, but definitely a huge part of the process, my beta readers. These are the people who love stories and are willing, and more than able, to tell me if my finished story is ready for you, my readers.